HANGMEN'S TRAIL

HANGMEN'S TRAIL

by

Jim Bowden

Dales Large Print Books
Long Preston, North Yorkshire,
BD23 4ND, England.

British Library Cataloguing in Publication Data.

Bowden, Jim
    Hangmen's trail.

    A catalogue record of this book is
    available from the British Library

    ISBN   978-1-84262-821-8 pbk

First published in Great Britain 1986 by Robert Hale Limited

Published in Large Print 2011 by arrangement with
Mr W. D. Spence

Dales Large Print is an imprint of Library Magna Books Ltd.

Printed and bound in Great Britain by
T.J. (International) Ltd., Cornwall, PL28 8RW

1

'Lieutenant Rogers!' The captain's voice carried above the bedlam of gunshots and curses, cut through the smoke and dust and pierced the cries of fear and pain.

From the protection of a boulder, Lieutenant Rogers glanced across the five-yard open space which separated him from his superior officer. 'Sir!'

All around them men lay dying, cut down without warning. Only a few moments had passed since the first shot took Captain Wesley in the shoulder, sending him reeling from his horse. Pandemonium had broken around the troop as volley after volley blasted into it from the boulder-strewn sides of the cutting through which the soldiers had been riding. Horses screamed, reared and went down in kicking heaps, soldiers dived for cover, grasped at bloody wounds or yelled in agony at shattered bones.

The surprise had been complete. Captain Wesley cursed himself for allowing vigilance to slacken, but there had been no reports of Confederate troops within fifty miles of the site of the ambush. They must have received information about the shipment of money and then filtered troops through Union-held land to try to prevent it swelling the funds of the Northern States.

The Captain saw that ten of his troopers had closed around the six pack-horses carrying the gold and that in spite of the roar of rifles and guns those horses were still under control.

'Rogers! Get that money to hell out of here. Don't let the bloody Feds take it!' The Captain's yells were accompanied by a vigorous waving of his arm in the direction of the pack-animals.

The Lieutenant took in the scene quickly. The men had got over their initial shock and from the cover of boulders and dead horses were answering shot with shot. Concerted firing from the Captain and the rest of the troop might just give him the chance he needed. He studied the lie of the land in one swift glance and figured his best line would be to follow the same direction as that taken by some of the frightened horses. If he acted quickly he would have some cover from the swirling dust-cloud created by their panicking hooves.

He looked back at the Captain and signalled that he was going. As he rose to his feet he heard the Captain yell for rapid firing. In a low, crouched run Lieutenant Rogers weaved towards the pack horses. Guns crashed in ear-splitting crescendo, filling the still air with stinking powder-fumes.

Ducking his body even further he concentrated his gaze on the group and its immediate surrounds. They needed horses and then an enormous amount of luck. He saw two of the troopers slammed backwards by the impact of rifle-bullets. Another fell clutching at his leg. Blood gushed, saturating the ground. Then he was among them.

'We're getting the money out of here!' he yelled. 'Scott, Marvin, horses!' As he turned he saw another trooper go down. He raced for two animals milling as they looked to escape from the frightening sounds which ripped the air. He grasped the reins and called to them with a soothing note as he turned them towards his men. Another horse was upon him. He grabbed and was almost jerked off his feet as he took the pull and brought it alongside the others. He urged them forward and saw that Scott and Marvin had both taken two horses. Seven. Enough.

'Mount up,' he yelled.

Troopers needed no second bidding to take this chance to escape. They guessed exactly what was in the Lieutenant's mind, and, once in the saddles, each grabbed the reins of a pack horse.

Lieutenant Rogers wheeled his horse. Dust swirled. His narrowed eyes saw that his men anticipated his intentions. He stabbed his horse into a gallop, flattening himself on the animal's back as it flew from the hell of the battle. Everything went into a moving blur with a few details impressed vividly in his mind. The pound of the horses behind him, the blood which oozed from the bullet furrow across his hand – a few more inches and he – men running up the hillside – Feds racing for their horses, pursuit. Then they were free of the whining bullets. Escape.

Lieutenant Rogers straightened in the saddle, checked his horse slightly and looked behind him. Six mounted men with six pack-horses were still with him. He eased the horse's gallop and, as he dropped back, he urged his men to keep up the pace. As the last pack-horse passed him he viewed the terrain behind them. A dust-cloud still marked their trail making it easy for the horsemen he saw galloping from the cutting to follow them.

He knew that the pack-horses would not be able to keep up the pace with which they had escaped and that it would only be a matter of time before their pursuers overhauled them.

He stabbed his horse into a fast run after his men, urging them to greater effort as he overtook them.

Twenty minutes later, dust-covered, sweating men and animals dropped into a shallow hollow. Lieutenant Rogers saw a chance and seized it. He hauled hard on the reins, yelling to his men to stop. Horses slithered, milled around and pulled at the hands which held them.

Rogers snapped his orders. 'Smith, Hurley, take all the horses out of this hollow.' He swung from his saddle and tossed his reins to Smith. 'The rest of you to the ridge.'

Men jumped to the ground and followed the Lieutenant up the slope, copying his crouch as they neared the top of the ridge. He signalled his men to stop. He dropped to his stomach and crawled the last few yards. The Confederate soldiers must have no inkling of what they were riding into.

He glanced back. Smith, Hurley and the horses were out of sight. He peered cautiously over the ridge. Ten riders. Thank goodness the Captain had held the others at the cutting. Rogers motioned to his four men to join him.

'Ten,' he whispered. 'Five of us. Two each. Hold your shots until you're certain. Let 'em come right up. Fire after I fire. They must be dead or we lose our chance to get away.'

Men, still breathing hard from the ride, licked their lips and nodded with a grim determination. They spread out, five yards between each man, and eased themselves into more comfortable positions. Every man was determined to make his one rifle-shot count.

Lieutenant Rogers glanced at them, checking that all were ready. He saw sweat-covered faces streaked with grime and powder of battle. One nervously bit his lip. With unsteady hand another wiped away the trickle of sweat before it impaired his vision. The third rested his forehead on his hand holding his rifle as if he was expecting this moment of unreality to pass as a dream.

The fourth's outwardly calm exterior did not betray the emotions churning inside him.

'Steady, men.' Lieutenant Rogers's whisper was firm to instil confidence. He raised himself so that he could just peer over the ridge. The riders were holding their horses in the full gallop of pursuit as they started towards the ridge. 'Keep down 'til I tell you!' he rasped when he caught a movement out of the corner of his eye.

Hooves pounded, their beat getting louder and louder, sending shock-waves through the ground, until each man thought his mind would burst with the noise and the discipline of keeping out of sight. Suddenly their world erupted.

'Now!' Lieutenant Rogers's yell shattered the tension.

Simultaneously four men rose a fraction after the Lieutenant. His shot was followed by a volley from the others. Five riders, stopped in their onward rush, crashed from their mounts.

Troopers swept their Colts from the ground as they leaped to their feet. Taken completely by surprise one more rider never had a chance to draw his gun. Then the four remaining horsemen were at the ridge and over it, hauling on the reins, clawing at their weapons. They spun their horses round. Guns blazed. A trooper went down, a bullet through his heart. Another got one through his throat. Two riders pitched to the ground. The other two urged their mounts back up the slope, bending low, intent on escaping from the nightmare which had hit them so suddenly.

Rogers read their intention. 'Stop 'em,' he screamed. Scot was sent flying, the impact of the charging animal breaking his neck and back. The two riders were over the ridge. 'Drop the horses!' yelled Rogers, a wild, half-insane screech to his voice.

He fired and saw his target crumble in its headlong gallop. Its rider pitched over its neck hitting the ground awkwardly with his shoulder. Almost at the same time Marvin

15

fired. The horse went on. For one brief moment Marvin thought he had missed. Then the horse plunged sideways, buckled and fell, pinning its rider by one leg. An agonising scream split the air as flesh and bone were crushed and ground by the weight and momentum.

Rogers straightened slowly from his crouching position. It seemed as if a lifetime had passed, but it had all happened quickly. A few seconds ago there were fifteen living beings, now there were four. The crescendo which had shattered the peace of the landscape was gone and stillness settled once again over the baked earth.

Rogers wiped his forehead and glanced at Marvin. 'Well done, trooper,' he said. 'Now, let's tidy up.' A steel edge had come to his voice.

He moved briskly towards the man who had been pitched from his horse and lay with one shoulder badly twisted under him. His face was creased by the pain which surged through him. Rogers stood over him, staring coldly for a moment.

'Help me.' The plea was gasped with an effort.

Rogers's face became the mask of an executioner. He raised his arm and took careful aim with his Colt. His eyes held an icy indifference, ignoring the young face which stared back with horror.

'No!'

The scream jerked at Marvin, immobilised by the shock of the Lieutenant's intention. Sure, they were at war, they had won a battle, but this was cold-blooded slaughter.

Marvin leaped forward and grasped the Lieutenant's arm. He swung it round away from the disabled soldier. 'Sir, you can't!' he shouted.

Rogers shook his arm free. His nostrils dilated, his eyes burned with a tense fury. 'Trooper, you forget yourself. I'll have you court-martialled for this.'

'But, sir, they're helpless.'

'They can talk,' snapped Rogers. 'We can't leave anyone to direct others on to our trail.'

'There may be no others.'

'I doubt that. Captain Wesley may have pinned some of them down but it's only a matter of time before our whole troop is wiped out. Then there'll be Feds after us.' Rogers started to turn towards the wounded man.

'But he's only a kid,' yelled Marvin.

The Lieutenant whipped round on Marvin. 'Youngster or not, he'd have killed us for the money,' he hissed.

Tension heightened between the two men. Their grimy, sweat-covered faces were masks of hostility.

'But–' started Marvin.

'No buts, trooper,' snapped Rogers. 'You're here to obey. I do the thinking.' A sardonic smile flicked his lips. 'And ordering. So get your gun and deal with that scum pinned under his horse.'

Marvin's mind reeled under the shock. He was no milksop and the war had brought him many horrors, but he baulked at cold-blooded killing of helpless men when it was

18

unnecessary. He saw an insane light in his officer's eyes. Rogers had a reputation for ruthlessness, but now it was as if he'd tasted blood and revelled in the killing.

Marvin straightened and eyed him fearlessly. 'No, sir!' he rapped.

Rogers's eyes flared. 'You refusing to obey an order, trooper?'

'It ain't necessary to kill them.'

Rogers fixed Marvin with an icy narrowing of his eyes. 'You're court-martialled here and now.' His voice rose. 'For refusal to obey an order on the field of battle: Guilty! Sentenced to be shot!' Rogers fired. From such close range he could not miss. Marvin, his eyes frozen in disbelief, was slammed backwards, dead before he hit the ground.

Rogers stared at the body, his lips curled in contempt. He turned to the injured soldier who was now shaking uncontrollably, scared out of his wits by what he had witnessed.

The Lieutenant stepped close. He gazed unfeelingly at the soldier. He raised his gun and fired.

Rogers swung round, hurried to the man pinned by his dead horse and without hesitation fired again. The wounded man jerked as the bullet smashed into him, but he felt no more pain.

As the sound died in the hollow, Rogers's gaze skimmed across the carnage around him. He grinned with a feeling of elation. He had won. He'd have won if there had been more, for he would have killed more. Silent forms were witness to the short, bloody action. The Confederates could not get on his trail now. Dead men could not testify as to the whereabouts of the money. Only he and two troopers would know. Two troopers. If they had been killed only he–

Rogers felt a power come with the thoughts. The destination of that money was in his hands. The war would not last forever. What then? What had he to go back to? Nothing. Just drifting, trying to find work with cattle. No command. No power. But if he–

Land. Acres. Cattle. Thousands. Men. A Crew.

A gentle breeze drifted through the hollow, brushed the bodies and cajoled Rogers's mind. He saw swaying grass across which stretched an endless line of cattle, moving steadily under the watchful eyes of a crew over which he had absolute authority. The vision could be his. Only two troopers were in his way!

He walked quickly to the rim of the hollow so that he could see the troopers and the horses. He waved, signalling them to come back up the slope. As he watched them his mind saw a future devoid of drifting from one job to the next.

'Bloody hell!' The two men gasped as one when they topped the rise and looked down into the hollow.

'It was, soldier, but we won,' said Rogers. 'We'll see to our own.'

'Won't the Feds be sending more after us?' Behind Smith's query was a hint that they should be moving.

Rogers's eyes flared. 'You questioning my judgement, soldier?' he snapped.

'No, sir.' The reply came sharp with the man's surprise at the Lieutenant's reaction.

Smith and Hurley exchanged glances and swung from their saddles. They knew what should be done. Identification taken from the blood-spattered corpses. They moved to their nauseating task. Rogers stepped behind them. He did not hesitate. His first bullet shattered a head, the second blasted a face as it half turned in shocked horror at what had happened. Silence returned to the hollow.

Now he was the only one!

He would be a man appalled by what had happened, dismayed at losing the money and distressed that he was the only survivor of a horrifying encounter which he had lost.

He stepped round the bodies and walked to the horses and the money.

2

The thickset man drew his horse to a halt on a rise close to the southern extremity of the Lazy A and let his gaze wander across the gentle slope to the river a mile away.

The scene always made him feel good for it was that river and its water-rights for which, five years ago, he had fought and won a range war with two brothers, new-comers to two ranches on the far side of the river.

Dan Fletcher eased his bulk in the saddle, drew a red kerchief from his pocket, pushed his stetson back and mopped the sweat from his forehead. He reached for his canteen and, as he tipped it to his mouth, he saw a lone rider put his horse into the water and slip from the saddle.

Dan hung the canteen from his saddlehorn and took out his spyglass. When he drew the stranger into focus he saw the man, who had his back to him, take off his bandana, soak it in the river, raise the horse's right foreleg and bathe it just above the hoof. The rancher lowered his spyglass, took a swig from his canteen, corked it and replaced it on the saddle-horn. He saw the man straighten and once more he trained his spyglass on him.

The stranger patted his horse on the neck, picked up the reins and started to lead the animal across the ford.

Dan levelled his gaze on the man's face. Suddenly he stiffened. 'It couldn't be. Not after eight years. And yet–? Dan studied the man again. He confirmed his identification.

'Cap Millet! What the hell are you doing here?' Dan hissed between tight lips.

He turned his horse quickly away from the top of the rise, swung from the saddle and crept back so that he could continue to watch the last man he had expected to see.

When Millet led his horse from the water

Dan saw that the horse was limping as if the foreleg was causing pain. He saw Cap survey the hillside and make for a hollow to his right.

As he watched, Dan Fletcher's mind sought a reason for Cap Millet being here. Though he tried to convince himself otherwise he kept returning to one fact – Millet was still searching, even after eight years. For what other reason could he be in this part of Texas? It was a big country. Why should he be here if the events of eight years ago were not upmost in Millet's mind? Millet was too close for comfort.

Dan pushed himself to his feet and hurried back to his horse. He removed his rifle from its scabbard and made his way along the hillside until he judged he was opposite the hollow to which he had seen Millet leading his horse. He crept cautiously to the top of the rise and saw that Millet had secured his horse under a tree on one side of the hollow. He studied him through his spyglass while the man made camp. When

Millet went to examine his horse, Fletcher was able to get a closer look at the animal's leg and he realised from what he saw that Millet would not be moving from this camp for a few days. In fact, never again. Fletcher picked up his rifle.

He raised it to his shoulder, eased himself more comfortably on the ground and took a line on Cap. It would be easy. Or would it? What about the sheriff? As these questions thundered into his mind, Dan lowered the rifle. He stared thoughtfully at the camp.

A dead man, shot, on Lazy A land, several of the ranch-hands knew he had ridden in this direction, a keen sheriff who wouldn't let go if he got the smallest of leads. Fletcher wanted no enquiries. Millet must be got rid of some other way.

Dan rubbed his chin thoughtfully. If he was to arrange Millet's death with no questions asked he would need help. But who? He could not involve his own men. They'd fight for him legal and out in the open but they were not the type to resort to a cold-blooded killing. Besides, they might want to know too much. The only way was to pay well for the job to be done with no reasons wanted or given.

Dan surveyed the camp, the horse and Millet, and once more felt sure that the man under surveillance would not be moving for a few days.

He slid away from the top of the rise and hurried to his horse.

When he reached the ranch buildings he rode over to his foreman, Jed Carson, who was supervising the breaking of some horses in a nearby corral.

'Jed, fix me a horse and some supplies,' he called. 'I'll be away about a week.'

3

The searing pain which tore through his body made Cap Millet wake with a start. He could not mistake the next blow from a boot driven hard into his side. He started to sit up, but another boot, this one spurred, pushed him back into the prone position and he found himself staring into the muzzle of a Colt .44.

'What the hell's this–' started Cap.

'Close it, horse-thief!' a voice cut in harshly.

Horse-thief? What the hell was this about?

His eyes focused beyond the Colt and took in a sharp-featured face from which dark eyes regarded him with cool contempt. A scar ran down the man's right cheek, and black hair showed from beneath the edges of a stained stetson pushed back on his forehead. Cap automatically imprinted the features in his mind, something he had trained himself to do from an early age when he had had to fend for himself after his parents had been killed in a bandit raid on their ranch. It was something he had sharpened during his service as a Union officer in the war between the States.

He turned his head slowly and saw three other men staring at him with looks which bode him no good.

Images impinged on his brain. A dirty, scruffy individual with a cast in his right eye who chewed on the end of an unlit cheroot. A forefinger of a left hand, missing at the knuckle, which constantly rubbed back and forth along a slit for a mouth while its owner peered at him from narrowed eyes. A short, stocky man who leered while he scraped at his fingernails with a knife which Cap reckoned he would have no hesitation in sticking into someone's ribs if he was displeased with them.

A more unsavoury bunch Cap had never

seen. He disliked the menace in their attitudes, and more particularly he did not relish the threat which was carried behind their word, horse-thief. It brought ugly visions of rough justice and a hangman's rope.

Cap turned his gaze back to the man with the gun and the spurred boots, signs Cap took as indicating that he was the leader or at least had some authority over the others. Maybe that came with the cruel streak Cap detected in his eyes.

'What do you mean, horse-thief?' Cap asked, keeping his voice razor-sharp.

'On your feet and find out,' answered the gunman. He stepped back a pace and, with the gun still threatening Cap, added, 'And do it real easy.'

Cap sat up slowly and turned the blanket back. He reached for his boots.

'You won't need those where you're going.' Cap glanced up and saw the man with the cheroot grinning at him, revealing tobacco-stained teeth. The man glanced at his stocky companion. 'Will he, Jake?'

'Sure won't, Dutch.' The man laughed and leered even more at Cap, as if anticipating a pleasure which was not going to be enjoyed by Cap.

Cap glanced back at the man with the gun. 'What do you say?' he asked quietly.

'Why ask me?' he countered.

'You have the authority there in your hand and I figure you've just got to say and these three sidekicks will jump to it,' replied Cap.

A touch of a smile flicked the man's lips. 'You've got me figured, mister. Hasn't he, Pecos?' He shot a quick glance at the man with the stub for a forefinger, and Cap reckoned that this was the one most likely to give the leader trouble.

'Sure, Cole, sure.' The words came sharp as if Pecos wanted to reassure him of his loyalty.

'There you have it, mister,' said Cole. 'And I say they've got it right. You won't need your boots.'

Cap climbed slowly to his feet. 'Horse-thief?' he queried. 'What you trying to pin on me?'

'Turn around, mister,' drawled Cole.

Cap eyed him for a moment then slowly did as he was told. His eyes widened with surprise, and he stifled the gasp which escaped as a hiss from between his tightened lips. Two horses were tethered on long ropes like his own.

He frowned, then swung round on Cole. 'What the hell is this?' he stormed, his eyes blazing angrily.

Cole stiffened. This man was lean and tall, but in his leanness there was a power which seemed to be held like a coiled spring ready to be unleashed, and, when it was, Cole reckoned this man would be a formidable adversary. He thrust his Colt more menacingly at Cap.

'Hold it!' he rapped. 'I could drop you before you moved an inch.'

'Well, what's this all about?' demanded Cap. 'I ain't a horse-thief. Those horses weren't there when I turned in last night.'

Dutch gave a harsh laugh. 'I suppose they just walked in and tied themselves? Have a heart, mister, we weren't born yesterday.'

'I know nothing about them,' hissed Cap.

''Course you deny it,' said Cole. 'But the evidence is there.'

Cap's mind whirled. He was in a tight spot. He could deny the accusation as much as he liked, but he realised it was only his word against theirs, and with the two horses in question tethered beside his own the evidence was against him.

'I'm telling the truth,' he rapped, staring hard at Cole.

'Who knows?' replied Cole casually.

'Whose horses are they?' asked Cap.

'One belongs to Jake and the other to me,' put in Pecos. 'They were taken yesterday.'

'Prove it,' challenged Cap, playing for time.

'Think we can't?' laughed Jake with the contempt of a man who knows he has the upper hand. 'Both have their left ears nicked. Take a look if you don't believe me.' He started to turn towards the horses.

'Sure I'll believe you,' said Cap, halting Jake. 'You wouldn't be accusing me if you weren't sure. I figure if they're your horses you must have planted them.' He eyed Cole. 'Why?'

'Let's cut the yabbering and get it over,' rasped Dutch.

Cole's three sidekicks glanced at him. He nodded. Dutch and Jake grabbed Cap's arms while Pecos positioned himself behind him. Cap resisted, but he felt the hard muzzle of a gun rammed into his back.

'You ain't got a chance, horse-thief,' Pecos hissed close to his ear. 'So quit resisting. You're going to swing and there ain't anything you can do about it.'

Cap stiffened in the vice-like grips of the men on either side of him. 'Why? Why did you plant those horses on me?' Though he tried to keep it from his voice a note of desperation had crept in. The vision of that rope was too near, and, at the mercy of four men, Cap could not see a way out. 'I've never set eyes on you before. I ain't done you any wrong. What's this all about?' He glanced desperately at Cole, Dutch and Jake in turn, seeking an answer, but he was only greeted with grim smiles.

'The tree,' rapped Cole. 'Watch him, Pecos.'

Cole holstered his gun and hurried to his horse. He unfastened a rope from around his saddlehorn, and, as he turned towards the tree, Cap saw that the rope was already shaped into a hangman's noose.

Cap struggled as the two men dragged him forward while Pecos prodded him in the back, but he could not break their firm grip.

'I'm innocent, and you know it!' he yelled, but no one took any notice of him. As much as he resisted and struggled he was relentlessly hustled towards the tree. Sweat broke out on his forehead and fear gripped his heart with ice-cold fingers. 'The law will get you for this. You can't get away with murder.'

'Who'll bother to try to prove it was murder when your body's found with a note fastened to you saying horse-thief? They'll figure you've got what you deserve.'

Cap knew he was right. These men would hang him for something he hadn't done and they'd get away with it.

With one last jerk, Jake and Dutch pitched him forward on to the earth beneath the tree. He hit the ground hard and stirred the dust as his hands slid forward. He rolled over on his back and found himself staring up at a noose as the rope was slung over the thick bough above him. He looked round wildly for some means of escape, but there was none. The four men ringed him, and the cold muzzle of Pecos's Colt was pointing menacingly at him.

'Get his horse, Jake,' ordered Cole.

As Jake hurried away, Cole turned to Dutch. 'Get ours,' he said.

Dutch hesitated and glanced apprehensively at Cap.

'It's all right, he ain't going to run,' said Cole drawing his Colt.

Dutch turned and strode quickly to their horses.

Cap licked his dried lips and glanced from Cole to Pecos and found only coldness in their eyes.

'You're making a big mistake,' he said. 'I'm here to meet three friends. They'll be along shortly and they'll lose no time in picking up your trail.'

Cole laughed derisively. 'Quit bluffing, Cap Millet.' He laughed again when he saw surprise show in Cap's eyes. 'Sure we know who you are. Captain in the Union Army in the war. Before that foreman at a ranch in Texas. Married a Southerner. She was killed during the war, and after the war you hunted down her killers. Since then you've drifted. You're a stranger to these parts. You ain't waiting for anyone. So on your feet.'

Millet's brain raced, trying to find some connection between himself and these men. If there was none how come they knew so much about him and why want to hang him?

'Where did you learn all this?' queried Cap.

'Does it matter? It won't help you when you're dangling from that rope.' Cole's voice and eyes went hard. 'Now get on your feet.'

Cap rose slowly, searching for an escape from the unsavoury end which faced him. Dutch and Jake were coming with the horses. He hadn't much time. But neither of the two guns relaxed for one second. He couldn't beat two of them.

'Right, Jake, tie his hands,' Cole ordered when Jake reached them with Cap's unsaddled horse.

Jake pulled Cap's hands roughly behind his back and quickly tied them with knots which Cap had no hope of forcing loose before the rope around his neck took his life.

'On your horse, Millet,' rapped Cole.

When Cap did not move Jake and Pecos grabbed him and, in spite of Cap's resistance, propelled him to the side of the animal.

His struggles were to no avail when the

two men gripped him firmly and raised him on to his horse's back. He had no option but to straddle. He knew if he deliberately fell he risked getting a bullet. Cole, his gun back in its holster, had moved to the horse's head and steadied the animal. For one brief moment Cap considered urging the animal into escape, but he noted that Pecos had drawn his gun again. He knew he would be dropped with a bullet in his back after he had gone only a few paces.

Jake hurried to give Dutch a hand with their horses, and when they had both mounted they ranged themselves on either side of Cap. Pecos holstered his gun, and he and Cole climbed into the saddles and moved close to Cap. Cole produced a piece of card strung with a loop which he slipped over Cap's head. The crudely scrawled words read, 'Horse-thief. We got him.'

A tight and sickening feeling gripped Cap's stomach. Beads of sweat stood out on his forehead. He was parched and looked at Cole with fear and pleading.

'Hold it,' he croaked. 'Maybe if I knew why you're doing this I could put things right.'

'They can't be put right,' said Cole quietly, and Cap saw no mercy in those cold eyes.

'Why? If only I knew why?' gasped Cap.

Their faces were grim. There was not a flicker of emotion amongst them.

'Give me some explanation,' yelled Cap.

All that came was a slight nod from Cole.

Immediately, Dutch and Jake let go riproaring yells and at the same time slapped Cap's horse hard across the rump. Startled by the unexpected, the animal, in its fright, sprang forward leaving Cap swinging at the end of the rope. It chaffed at his neck and tightened round his throat. He tried to gulp, but couldn't. The pressure increased. Blood pounded in his brain and he was unaware of what was happening around him.

The other horses had been equally startled by the shattering outbreak of noise and had leaped forward into a run with Cap's horse. Their riders held them under control, but with Cole's shout of 'Let 'em run,' they allowed the animals sufficient freedom.

'What about Millet?' yelled Pecos as he closed his mount nearer Cole. 'Hadn't we better be sure?'

'He's as good as dead,' shouted Cole. 'Let's get to hell out of here,' and he kept riding.

None of the horsemen looked back as they topped the rise. They dropped over the ridge which put the swinging man beyond their gaze.

Cap swayed at the end of the rope. His brain roared like a mighty waterfall as the rope tightened round his throat. This was it. This was the end. What a way to die. Choked to death at the end of a rope for something he didn't do. His mind began to swim. Then a sound penetrated. A beating. Cap tried to force himself to take it in.

Hoofbeats. A voice. Imagination? Someone. A body near him. An arm around his shoulders. The swaying stopped. A swish of something through the air above his head. A momentary pull of the rope against his neck. The pressure gone. Falling. Falling. A thud. He felt little of his contact with the ground, and then he was aware of its firmness, of its support rather than that of the rope.

'You'll be all right.' The voice was dim and distant as if from a dream. It wasn't real. It couldn't be. He was dead, in another world.

Yet he sensed a body beside him. A tugging at the ropes which held his hands. A voice quiet and gentle, reassuring, but he was unable to make out the words. He swallowed, gasping, trying to get rid of the choking feeling. It was a relief to have no pressure around his throat and to feel life flowing slowly back instead of away. His hands were free, and automatically they came to the rope around his neck. He felt other hands there, easing the rope and taking it gently over his head.

Then it was gone, and he lay prone on his back, gulping air, enjoying being alive. No one spoke. There must have been someone. He didn't get out of that noose by himself.

He forced his eyes open.

He stared upwards. Everything was a blur. He blinked, trying to bring something into focus. His mind whirled and spun. He closed his eyes. Then everything seemed to explode. He opened his eyes wide and the face of a young man came sharp and clear.

Cap's gaze was met with a warm, reassuring look.

'That sure was a close thing, mister, but I reckon you'll live. Maybe have a rope-burn on your neck for some time, if not for always, but I reckon that's better than being dead.'

Cap sat up, fingering his neck as he did so. 'I'm mighty grateful to you' he said thrusting out his right hand. 'Cap Millet's the name.'

The young man took Cap's hand in a firm grip. 'Pete Wells. Card says you're a horse-thief.' He nodded at the card which he had thrown on the ground.

'Then why did you cut me down?'

'Don't go for this rough justice. There's a

law to deal with such things.'

'I'm mighty glad you have such prin-
ciples.'

'Are you a horse-thief?' Pete demanded,
his eyes fixed intently on Cap.

Cap stopped fingering his neck and
looked up at Pete with a slight inclination of
his head. 'Do you figure I am?' he asked.

'Well–' Pete hesitated as if trying to weigh
up the situation– 'I see only one horse and
your night camp. I reckon you were jumped
while you were asleep. But there are no
horses you could have stolen. But then I
reckon whoever strung you up, would take
them.' He paused.

'Right,' agreed Cap. 'But I figure you've
been weighing me up. What have you made
out?'

'Well, you don't look like a horse-thief,'
replied Pete.'

'Good,' said Cap, pushing himself to his
feet. 'And you're right. I ain't.'

'Then what's it all about?' asked Pete, a
frown furrowing his brow.

'Wish I knew,' replied Cap. 'Like you said I was jumped while I was asleep. Four of them. Never set eyes on them before. They accused me of stealing two of their horses. Sure enough there were two horses tethered along with mine. Don't know why they went to that trouble; maybe looked right if anyone happened along. They came prepared, had that card ready. It sure was a frame-up, but don't ask me why. I've no answer.'

'Did they know you?' queried Pete as they walked to Cap's bedroll.

'Yeah, they sure did, gave me a brief history of my life.'

'Yet you didn't know them.'

'No.'

'You ain't from around these parts,' commented Pete. 'What about them? Can you describe them?'

'Sure. Cole appeared to be the leader, had a scar down his right cheek, cruel look in his eyes and he wore spurs. Dutch was dirty and scruffy, chewed on a cheroot. Jake was short and stocky, toyed with a knife. Pecos–'

'A man with a stub for a fore-finger,' broke in Pete.

'You know them!' There was excitement in Cap's voice. 'They're from round here?'

'No. Not now. They were about five years ago. Bad bunch. Things got a bit hot for them and they cleared out. Nobody knew where. I'm surprised they've come back.'

'You seen 'em around recently?' asked Cap as he sat down and reached for his boots.

'No.' Pete's reply was emphatic.

'Right,' said Cap. 'I want those hombres. I want 'em bad, but I reckon it won't be easy to pick up their trail right now and I sure don't feel like riding yet, so tell you what, Pete, let's put some coffee on and you can tell me what you know about them. Anything which will help me get 'em 'cos they're sure going to pay for what they did this morning after I find out why they did it.'

4

'You're from around these parts, I guess,' said Cap, glancing at Pete who had sat on his right when the coffee and food were ready.

'Yes, Pa has the Running W. Say, why don't you come back with me, rest up a while? You can't be feeling too good after your experience.'

'Thanks, but I'll be fine after a cup of coffee, bit of grub and a rest while I have them. Now, let's hear what you have to say.'

'They rode in about six years ago.' Pete paused as if doubting his own statement, then added, 'Yes, it would be, I was sixteen at the time. They rode as gun-slingers for a man called Fletcher, Dan Fletcher.'

'Why did he want four gun-slingers?'

'He owned the Lazy A, still does. He was having trouble with a couple of neighbours.'

'What sort of trouble?' queried Cap.

'Water-rights,' Pete explained. 'Led to something of a local range war. Pa wasn't involved. Concerned the far side of Fletcher's ranch from us. Trouble lasted about a year, but the four gun-slingers cleared it up in Dan Fletcher's favour. Rumour had it at the time that they had some mighty persuasive powers.'

Cap grunted, reaching for the coffee-pot. 'Not much for me to go on. Never heard of this Fletcher.'

'Don't suppose you have if this is the first time you've been around Claystone,' Pete pointed out. 'You won't have heard of Pa either.'

Cap shook his head as he poured the coffee. 'That's right,' he agreed. He passed a cup to Pete. 'Know anything more about Fletcher's gun-slingers?'

'No. The disputes were suddenly settled and they were gone. No one knew where or cared. Ain't heard of them from that day to this.'

'No one seen 'em around during the last few days?'

'Not that I know of.'

'Figure you would have?' asked Cap.

'Sure, I've been in town. If anyone had seen 'em they'd have been talked about.'

'So it looks as if they've been lying low,' mused Cap.

'Yeah, but why?' Pete puzzled.

'Wish I knew the answer to that.' Cap scratched his chin thoughtfully.

'Looks as though they were laying for you,' suggested Pete.

'Sure looks that way,' agreed Cap. 'But if that was the case how did they know I was here?'

'They been trailing you?' said Pete.

'I figure I'd have known.' Cap paused thoughtfully. 'But suppose they had, then they could have jumped me any time. Why wait until now? I've been here four days, since my horse went lame. He's all right now and I was going to move on today.'

'It sure looks as if they were out to get you,'

grunted Pete. 'Sorry I'm not much help.'

Cap smiled wryly. 'Help? You only saved my life.'

'I meant with information.'

'You've probably helped more than you know,' said Cap. 'You've identified them and you've given me what I hope will be a starting-point.'

'Starting-point?' Pete looked puzzled.

'Dan Fletcher,' explained Cap. 'He hired 'em so maybe he can tell me more about them.'

'Sure hope so,' said Pete. 'I wish you all the luck. If you're this way again look us up.'

'Thank,' said Cap as they stood up. 'I sure will.' He shook hands with Pete firmly. 'And thanks again for saving my life. I'll always owe you.'

Cap watched the young man ride away, and for a moment wished he was back at that age, but then he remembered that, if he was, there would be the horrors of the war and his wife's murder still to face.

He busied himself breaking camp and

getting ready for what might be a long trail, but of one thing he was certain; he would not give up until he found the would-be hangmen and learned the truth.

His horse had calmed and stood a short distance away champing at some grass. Cap retrieved the animal and soon had it saddled. He quickly stowed his gear, and once in the saddle he headed for the Lazy A.

When the ranch came in sight he slowed his pace.

The main building was long and low and fronted by a verandah. A short distance to the right stood a building which Cap judged to be the bunkhouse, and beyond that was a third building which was obviously the stables. Close by were six large corrals and four smaller ones. In one of these four cowboys were working some mustangs.

The whole place was well kept and had an air of a solid, hard-working ranch. He saw a man come out of the house and watch him from the verandah.

Cap judged the man to be about twenty-five. He was well built, solid, giving the impression of strength. Cap figured he was a man who could handle himself and that the sharp eyes would not miss a thing.

'Dan Fletcher about?' queried Cap as he halted his horse.

'No. I'm Jed Carson, his foreman.'

'I'd like to see Mr Fletcher.'

'You can't, he's away. Won't be back for a few days.' Jed saw suspicion come to Cap's eyes as he looked beyond the foreman to the front door. Jed laughed. 'You figure Mr Fletcher's in there 'cos I was and I'm only the foreman?'

'Something like that,' replied Cap.

'Mr Fletcher treats me like his son since his own got killed in some troubles we had a few years ago.'

Cap nodded. Jed's voice had a ring of truth in it.

'I'm Cap Millet. It's about those troubles I wanted to see Dan Fletcher. Maybe you can help?'

'Step down,' invited Jed.

Cap swung smoothly from the saddle and stepped on to the verandah.

'What's your interest in something which happened and was settled five years ago?' asked Carson.

'THAT.' Cap pulled down his neckerchief.

'Rope-burn,' gasped Jed. 'And it ain't very old.'

'Right,' said Cap as he readjusted his neckerchief.

'And what's that got to do with our troubles?'

'Four men jumped me while I was asleep. Accused me of horse stealing and put me at the end of a rope without an explanation as to why they'd framed me. Fortunately for me they rode off as soon as I was swinging. Then, even more fortunate for me, a young fella, name of Pete Wells, rode up and cut me down.'

'Can't see what this has to do with the troubles,' put in Jed.

'Pete Wells was able to identify the men from my description,' said Cap.

'From these parts?' asked Jed.

'No. But Pete said they were here six years ago and stayed about a year. He said they rode for Fletcher. Gun-slingers. Cole and his sidekicks, Pecos, Dutch and Jake.'

Cap's announcement startled Jed. 'You sure? They ain't been heard of since they left here.'

'I described 'em and you must admit there'd be no mistaking a description of those bastards,' replied Cap.

'Reckon not,' agreed Jed. 'Pete was only a youngster at the time but he was a bright kid. He'd know 'em from a description. You known 'em before?'

'No,' answered Cap. 'First time I set eyes on them was when they kicked me awake this morning.'

'Why you if you didn't steal their horses?'

'That's what I'd like to know,' said Cap, 'and that's what I aim to find out. I have a strong feeling they were working for some-one.'

'Meaning Mr Fletcher?' Jed's eyes flared.

'Hold hard,' rapped Cap. 'I ain't accusing him. I don't know him, and as far as I know he has no connection with my past. But I figure on finding these men and, when Pete said they used to ride for Mr Fletcher, I hoped he might be able to tell me something about them which would give me a starting point.'

Carson grunted. 'Don't know that I can help much. Like I said, I ain't heard of these four since they left.'

'But you can tell me what they're like, where they came from, where they're likely to be? Fletcher brought them in as gunslingers 'cos he was having trouble with neighbours over water-rights. They were four mean men, Carson; the situation must have been grim for Fletcher to employ suchlike. How did he know them? How did he find them? Anything might help me to track them down.'

'Sure, we had a rough time,' explained Jed. 'Mr Fletcher pioneered this ranch, built it up from a run-down thing he bought after the war. But he wasn't lucky with neighbours when two brothers moved in on the other side of the river. It wasn't long before their intentions to take over the area were clear. Mr Fletcher clashed over water-rights. If he'd given an inch he'd have suffered. He stuck out, and they brought in some gun-toters. Mr Fletcher figured he'd meet them with the same. He had a good crew, they'd have done anything for him, but once professional gunmen were here he figured his crew needed some protection. Cole and his sidekicks proved their worth. They weren't men the Lazy A usually employed, but they were what we needed then. Like you said they were a mean bunch. They rode rough but they got a job done.'

Cap nodded. 'How did you come by them?' he asked.

'One of our newest hands, he'd been with us about a year, came from the north, had heard of them around Durango. When Mr Fletcher put the idea of bringing in gunslingers to the crew, Clem told him about them. So he sent Clem to Durango with a deal for them.'

'You figure Durango's their usual hang-out?' asked Cap.

'Can't be certain,' replied Jed. 'Only know that that was where Clem had heard of them.'

'Can I have a word with Clem?' Cap requested.

''Fraid not. Clem died alongside Mr Fletcher's boy in the troubles.'

'There's no reason for you to bring 'em back at the present?' Cap put his question tentatively.

Jed frowned, reading more into the implication than Cap intended. 'Meaning what?'

'No offence meant,' Cap quickly reassured the foreman. 'I'm just trying to find a reason for those hombres being around here when I was.'

Jed grunted. 'We've no reason to have them back. Everything's peaceable now and we have good neighbours. Can't think why they should be back here.'

'Then it looks as if they were here to get me,' mused Cap. 'But why? And why here?'

'Can it be in the reason why you're in these parts?' suggested Jed.

Cap shook his head. 'Been working way down in the south-east. Job finished so I figured I'd head north and west aways. Horse went lame so I rested up. Been around for four days. I'd have moved on today. If those hombres had been following me they could have jumped me any time. They didn't so I figure they weren't.'

'You mean they came here with the purpose of getting you?' said Jed, a touch of disbelief in his voice. 'But how could they know you were here?'

'I don't know. Unless somebody told them.'

'Do you know anyone around here?'

'No, first time in these parts.' Cap frowned. 'It's sure got me puzzled.'

'I wish I knew some way to help you,' said Jed.

'You have. I'd hoped for more, but at least you told me they were hired in Durango.

Maybe I can pick up a lead there.'

'Could do,' agreed Jed, 'but watch how you go. Durango's a place for suchlike. Place never came to anything, left half finished, no law there and none would ride in, so hard cases found it a useful place to hole up for a while. You'll need eyes in the back of your head.'

5

As anxious as he was to reach Durango, Cap did not press his horse. He did not want it going lame again and he needed to gain strength after his harrowing experience.

He constantly recalled the physical appearances of the four men so that, when he saw them, there would be instant recognition, for he knew it could make all the difference between life and death. They would expect him to be dead, so he would have the element of surprise, but their shock would be short and recovery would be quick. Cap knew he would have to outplay them and, in those few seconds of surprise, he would have to reduce the odds of four to one.

Thirty-six hours later, with Durango in sight, Cap found a low rise, a short distance from the town, from which he could study it through his spyglass.

Three streets ran parallel with each other, the middle one being twice as wide as the others. These were crossed by four roads and the grid they formed was filled with an assortment of buildings of all shapes and sizes. The town had a dilapidated air about it as if it was a place which had never developed to the hoped-for possibilities of its first erectors.

Having taken in a general survey, Cap eased his stetson, wiped the sweat from his brow and wished the mid-afternoon sun would lose some of its intensity. He guessed it was that heat which gave the town a look as if it was deserted, for there was no sign of movement, not even along the main street.

Cap waited a moment trying to decide his next course of action. Then, his mind made up, he sent his horse slowly down the slope and kept to the same pace across the flat towards the town.

He made for the main street, and, as he rode slowly along it, his eyes searched, taking in every detail. A saloon lay on his right-hand side about halfway along the rickety sidewalk which was in need of repair in several places The left-hand sidewalk was no better and was flanked by a store, a hotel which had seen better days, and a livery stable where a short, bearded man, with a hat pulled down over his eyes, lounged on a chair in the shade of the doorway.

By the time Cap reached the stable he knew he had been noted by three men who idled on chairs outside the saloon, but none of them made any movement.

Cap, amused by the snores which came from the sleeping man, pulled up outside the stable. He swung from the saddle smoothly and stepped quietly to the chair. He leaned forward until his mouth was close to the man's ear. 'Stable's on fire!' he rapped sharply and stepped back.

The man came wide awake with a gasp of alarm and struggled to jump to his feet.

'What! How!' His eyes were wide with horror. Cap's grinning face came into his vision and with it the fact that there were no flames or smoke. The small man thrust his neck forward, his eyes narrowing as he glared at Cap. 'Why you low-down, good-for-nothing coyote,' he spluttered.

'Hold hard,' Cap got in quickly before the bearded man really erupted. 'Want to earn a couple of dollars?'

'You damned foo–' the words spluttered to a halt. The man's eyes widened. 'Two dollars?' he gasped.

'Sure,' grinned Cap. 'Maybe even double it.'

'Double it?' The man swallowed hard. 'Ain't seen that sort of money in one payment in years. What you want, young fella?' All the anger and threat had gone and in their place was a desire to oblige.

'Look after my horse for one thing and some information for another.'

'Information?' The man eyed Cap suspiciously.

'Yeah, and seeing as how we're going to talk, let's exchange names.'

'Rusty Parks,' grunted the stableman.

'Cap Millet,' returned Cap. 'The horse, Rusty, we can talk while you take care of it.'

Rusty took the reins and spoke quietly to the animal as he led it to the nearest stall. Cap noted the animal's response to the gentle voice and he knew his horse was in the hands of a man who loved horses. Cap leaned against the stall in a position from which he could keep the doorway in view.

'When will you want this horse again?' asked Rusty as he started to take off the saddle.

'Depends on what I learn from you,' replied Cap. 'Give him a good rub down, a feed and have him saddled ready to ride at a moment's notice.'

Rusty paused as he grasped the saddle to lift it from the horse's back. 'You expecting trouble?' he asked, eyeing Cap with a quizzical curiosity.

'Maybe,' replied Cap.

'Then you've sure come to the right place to find it,' commented Rusty as he proceeded with his job.

'What do you mean?' queried Cap.

'This town had the makings at one time but the prospects fizzled out. A lot of people moved away, the law moved out, wasn't worthwhile keeping a lawman here, so, when word got round, all the scum you could imagine drifted in and out of here. Still do. Use it to hole up for a few hours, a few days, weeks or longer, just as the fit takes them. There's been some rough, tough men through here, and I tell you, Mister Cap, you watch your step if you're staying, unless you're one of them.' He paused in his rubbing and eyed Cap. 'And I guess you aren't, so heed my words.'

'Thanks for the warning,' said Cap. 'You run with them?'

A touch of annoyance flared in Rusty's eyes as he flashed a look at Cap. 'Hell, no. I'd want my head examining if I did.'

'Then why did you stay here?' quizzed Cap.

'I was doing all right when the town began

to run down. I didn't know what to do, but I'd got tired of moving on, been doing it all my life. I figured I'd got settled for my last few years, so I said what the hell and stayed. I still keep my stable going, but it ain't the same as it used to be. The scum that come in here aren't particular about paying and they aren't the sort to argue with.' Rusty grimaced and gave a resigned shrug of his shoulders.

'But you get to know most of what's happening around here,' suggested Cap.

Rusty chuckled deep in his throat. 'Sure do,' he agreed, 'sure do. You looking for someone?' He poured out some grain for the horse.

'Yes.'

'I knew it,' said Rusty with a low laugh. 'It figured, or you wouldn't have ridden in here. And anyone who saw you will figure the same. Who you looking for?'

'Four gun-slingers who ride together,' started Cap.

Rusty let out a low whistle. 'Four? You sure

are stacking up the odds.'

'I figure I can handle them,' said Cap.

Rusty raised an eyebrow and gave a soft chuckle as he said, 'I wouldn't be surprised if you can. Who are they?'

'Only know their first names,' said Cap. 'Cole's the leader, Pecos, Dutch and Jake his sidekicks.' Before he had finished, Cap realised from the look on Rusty's face that he knew them.

Rusty let out another low whistle of surprise. 'You sure know how to pile the trouble on. You couldn't have picked four worse characters to tangle with. How'd you come to be up against those four-flushers?'

'That,' said Cap and eased his neckerchief so that Rusty could see his neck.

Rusty gasped when he looked up from the hoof he was examining. 'How'd you get that?'

'Cole and his sidekicks tried to hang me, day before yesterday.'

'Hell! What for?'

'Don't know. Said I'd stolen their horses. It

70

was a frame-up, but I couldn't find out why. Young fella name of Pete Wells cut me down, just in time. He recognised the four men from my description. Said they'd ridden as gunmen for a rancher, name of Fletcher, five, six years ago. I visited Fletcher to try to get a lead on them, but he was away. His foreman didn't know why they were around Claystone. He hadn't heard of them since they left after doing the job for his boss. All he could tell me was that they were hired in Durango. So here I am. I want those bastards.'

'You won't find them here,' commented Rusty. 'Rode out, yesterday. Flush with money.'

'That's interesting,' said Cap thoughtfully. 'Could have been paid to do that job on me.'

'Any idea who by?' asked Rusty.

'No. It's a real puzzler,' replied Cap with a shake of his head. 'You look after their horses while they were here?'

'Yeah.'

'Did you hear where they were going?'

'Nope. But I heard Cole say he'd see the others in a week, and they took the north trail.'

'Could have been splitting up.' mused Cap, 'or maybe just Cole going on his own. Do you think I might get a lead in the saloon?'

'It's possible. But be careful what you say. They've friends around here.'

'Sure will.' Cap nodded and made for the door. He paused to glance through the opening. The street was just as it had been when he rode into town.

He glanced back at Rusty, who was watching him, and caught the concern on the stableman's face. Cap raised his hand and stepped into the sunlight. He blinked against its strength and strolled along the street.

'Howdy,' he greeted casually when he reached the men sitting outside the saloon, but received only nods in reply. He moved to the batwings of the saloon which squeaked as he pushed them open.

He found himself in an oblong room in which the wall directly opposite to him was occupied by a bar, the most solid and finest piece of furnishing in the room. It almost looked out of place in the shabby, run-down surroundings. Sawdust was strewn across the floor. Several tables occupied one end of the room while the other contained a few gambling-tables. He guessed that the space between was used for some sort of fifth-rate entertainment if ever it was called for. A stairway at one end of the bar ran up to a balcony which gave access to a number of rooms.

Half a dozen men lounged against the bar while several others were seated at the tables, and a card-game was in progress at the only gaming-table in use.

Three saloon girls, who were looking down from the balcony with disinterest, brightened and moved towards the stairs when they saw the stranger enter the saloon.

Cap took this all in, as he strolled casually to the bar, while outwardly he seemed to be showing little interest in his surroundings. He leaned on the bar and quickly assessed the barman who eyed him with curiosity. Cap judged him to be a man who would run with whoever suited his needs best.

'Beer,' requested Cap.

The man nodded and drew the necessary liquid. 'Stranger in Durango,' he commented as he pushed the foaming glass towards Cap.

'Yeah,' replied Cap, tossing a coin on to the bar. 'Passing through.'

'Where you from?' queried the barman. Cap judged he was getting the routine questions put to any stranger who came to this town. He knew the information would quickly circulate among the less savoury characters putting them on the alert until the stranger was cleared to their satisfaction, which meant no threat to their freedom.

'Drifting,' replied Cap.

'Must have been somewhere before you hit Durango,' commented the barman, a slight edge coming to his voice.

'Sure, like everyone,' replied Cap testily.

'Come, mister, being a bit edgy, aren't you? We can soon cure that, can't we, girls?' The voice came huskily from Cap's left as one of the saloon girls slid beside him and cast her comment to the other two who came to the bar on Cap's right.

'Guess you could at that,' smiled Cap as his glance took in all three, 'but not now, I've some business to attend to. Maybe you can help.' He looked at the barman. 'Give them what they want.'

The barman knew their drinks without asking, and as he poured them out Cap directed his next query at the three girls. 'I'm trying to get in touch with four fellas I knew way back. I was told I might find them in Durango.'

'Can't help you if we don't know their names,' laughed one of the girls as she reached for the glass the barman pushed across the counter.

'Only knew them as Cole, Pecos, Dutch and Jake. Never knew their second names.'

Serious expressions suddenly wiped the smiles from the saloon girls' faces, and Cap noted the sharp exchange of looks between the girl on his left and her two companions.

'You a friend?' she asked suspiciously.

'I want to get in touch with them about a job,' replied Cap evasively.

'That could be taken two ways, mister,' said the girl guardedly. 'You the law?'

'Would I be in Durango if I was? I figure you'd smell a lawman a mile off. He wouldn't stand a chance. No, I'm not the law. I heard tell they did a good job around Claystone five or six years ago.'

'You want them to do a similar job for you?'

Cap realised that the girl's suspicions had not been completely allayed. 'Are they in town?' he asked, avoiding her question. Although he knew the answer he did not want them to know that he had already questioned someone. He was aware that one of the girls on his right had moved away and was talking to two men further along the bar.

'No,' came the reply.

'Know where they are?'

'No.'

'Have they been here recently?' queried Cap.

'Not for some time,' the girl lied.

Cap nodded. 'That's a pity. It could have meant money for them.'

But the girl was not to be drawn, and he wondered if this was a special loyalty to the four men. Was their recent job known to the lawless community in Durango? Were these girls suspicious that someone had got on their trail to bring them to justice for the hanging? Cap recalled Rusty's warning. If he had not convinced these saloon girls he knew he would have to be on his guard.

'Sorry, we can't be of more help,' the girl said with a finality which indicated that she had no more to say on the subject. 'And I guess if you aren't interested in anything else we'll drift.' Cap noticed a slight inclination of the head, a sign which her companion had taken, for both girls moved away from him. Cap noticed the third girl leave the men to whom she was talking and join the other two at one of the tables.

Cap drained his glass, nodded to the barman and left the saloon. He paused momentarily on the sidewalk, then walked past the men lounging outside and headed for the livery stable.

Cap heard the squeak of the batwings behind him followed by footsteps on the sidewalk. The briskness in the noise ceased suddenly and Cap guessed that the two men had stepped off the sidewalk on to the roadway. He half glanced over his shoulder, but it was sufficient for him to identify the two men to whom one of the saloon girls had gone while he was talking to the others.

Cap was alert to being followed, but when he turned off the sidewalk to cross the street the two men were nowhere to be seen. The tension in him eased a little. Maybe he had been wrong. But he remained alert, suspicious that those two particular men should have left the saloon so soon after he had done so.

Cap reached the livery stable, opened the door and stepped inside and immediately regretted his lack of caution as the hard muzzle of a Colt dug into his side.

'Sorry, Cap, couldn't warn you,' called Rusty who faced a gun held unerringly at his middle.

Cap recognised the two men from the saloon.

'What you want with Cole?' hissed the man who poked his Colt harder into Cap's side.

'Reckon you were told in the saloon,' replied Cap, regathering his composure.

'You tell me,' snapped the man.

'Have a proposition to put to him.'

'What about?'

'For his ears alone.'

'What about?' rapped the man. There was a threat behind the tone. These men would get to know one way or another and it was up to Cap to take the painless way out.

'You a friend of Cole's?' asked Cap.

'Yeah. And I didn't like the way you were nosing about him. So talk.'

Cap hesitated. He couldn't be sure whether these two men had a genuine interest in protecting Cole or whether they were just trying to knuckle in on what might be a lucrative proposition.

'I want him and his sidekicks to do a job for me. I'll pay well, you too if you can tell me where he is.'

'What's the job?'

'Where's Cole?' countered Cap.

'You tell me the job and I'll figure whether he'll be interested.'

Cap cast a glance at Rusty and he saw that the stableman was alert to any possibility of extracting themselves from this situation.

'Well, if you reckon he won't be, you two might be interested. Say, that's not a bad idea. Save all the trouble of contacting Cole wherever he may be.'

'Could be,' replied the man, a little of the hostility going from his voice. 'He's a couple of days' ride from here, so maybe we'll do the job instead. What is it?'

'Concerns gold. Partner and I want some protection when we move it.'

At the mention of gold Cap saw a gleam come to the man's eyes and he noted that his crony half turned from Rusty.

'Sounds the job for us, Ed.'

'Sure does, Hal,' agreed the other with a marked enthusiasm.

'Where is this gold and where you moving it to?' asked Hal.

'Show you better on a map. I've got one in my saddlebag.' Cap started to move.

'Hold it!' rapped Hal. 'We'll do this easy like.' He eyed Cap, threatening him with the consequences should this be a trick. He motioned with his gun.

Cap moved to the stall where Rusty had stabled his horse. He unfastened the saddle-bag and was about to reach inside when Hal stopped him with a harsh, 'Leave it.' He motioned Cap to one side.

Cap did so and stepped back in the same movement. He cast a quick glance at Rusty and Ed. Although Ed still held his gun on Rusty, Cap saw that some of his interest was on Hal.

Hal, keeping his gun on Cap, stepped forward to the saddlebag. He reached inside and felt around. His face darkened with the surprise he had received and for one moment his whole attention was diverted to the saddlebag as he started to say, 'There's no–'

Cap seized that moment. He moved swiftly, crashing his fist deep into Hal's side and driving him hard against the side of the stall. At the same time he grabbed Hal's gun-hand and forced it upwards. He brought his knee up into the man's groin, and as Hal buckled, with the breath driven from his body, Cap swung the hand holding the gun hard across the wooden partition. Hal's grip was broken and the gun fell to the earth floor. One more blow pitched him into unconsciousness.

Rusty, having judged from Cap's exchange of looks that he was a man who would seize the half-chance, moved the moment that he saw Cap's action had taken Ed's attention. In that split second Rusty kicked hard at the man's shin and at the same time knocked his gun-hand sideways. Taken off his balance Ed had no chance to avoid Rusty's head as the stableman butted him hard in the face. Ed staggered backwards, and Rusty went with him pitching him on to the floor. As they hit the earth Rusty grabbed Ed's wrist forcing him to keep the gun turned away. As he battled against Rusty's grip, Ed was helpless when Cap kicked the gun from his hand, and he had no protection when Rusty butted him once again, this time with sufficient force to send his mind reeling into oblivion.

'Well done, Rusty,' praised Cap as he dragged the stableman to his feet.

Rusty grunted. 'Don't like fellas using my stable for their dirty work.' He glanced at the two unconscious forms. 'Guess I'll have to leave Durango now. Sure must be off my head to help a fella I don't know much about.'

'Must have liked what you saw,' grinned

Cap. 'Reckon you'd better ride along with me.'

'Reckon so, I ain't anything else better to do. And maybe you'll need my help again.'

'Shouldn't be surprised. Let's tie these two hombres up. We don't want 'em found too soon.'

The two men quickly had Hal and Ed securely bound and gagged. They took them to an empty stall in the far corner of the stable and threw some straw over them.

Once their horses were ready and Rusty had collected his belongings, Rusty put the question, 'Where to?'

'Head north. That's the direction you said Cole and his sidekicks took. Hal said they were two days' ride away, so you think about that.'

The two men left the stable by the rear door in order to keep off the main street and away from prying eyes. They were soon clear of the town and heading along the north trail.

6

They rode at a brisk pace away from Durango wanting to put as much distance between them and the town as quickly as possible without overtiring the horses.

'You figured anything?' queried Cap when they had settled to the ride.

'Two days would take them to Mather, provided they didn't deviate.'

'Cole was going to see the others in a week. Maybe he's there or the other three. Maybe that's where they're meeting. Know what sort of a place this Mather is?'

'Ordinary small town. Can't figure any reason for Cole and his sidekicks to go there.'

Cap nodded and lapsed into a thoughtful silence.

Two days later, with Mather in sight, Cap

called a halt. 'You figure you can do some nosing?'

Rusty grinned. 'Sure. What you got in mind?'

'If any of them are there I don't want them to see me yet. If they come across you it wouldn't matter, you could be in Mather for any number of reasons.'

'Sure, I'll look the place over.'

'I'll make camp among those rocks,' said Cap, indicating a position off the trail. He took Rusty's belongings and watched the older man ride off.

It was late afternoon when Cap saw Rusty returning across the flat land, his figure distorted by the shimmering air rising with the heat of the sun.

'Learn anything?' asked Cap anxiously when Rusty slipped from his horse.

'Sure did,' replied Rusty with a grin. 'Cole isn't there but the others are.'

'Good,' rasped Cap, pleased that he was near his would-be hangmen.

'They're spending big.'

'Money paid for the job of hanging me.'

'Maybe,' said Rusty. 'What happens when that's all gone?'

'Suchlike don't think that far ahead. They spend while they have it and let the devil take care of them after that.'

'Sure, but I figure there's more to it than that. I reckon some of that money is being put to special use.'

'In what way?'

'Well, I located them in the saloon. Kept out of sight. They were spending freely. Then Dutch leaves the other two so I follow him hoping he might lead me to Cole if Cole was around. He met a man in an alley two blocks from the saloon. He gave the man some money.'

'So?' prompted Cap when Rusty paused.

'Well, this was a meeting that wasn't supposed to be seen by anyone else. It was brief. A few words were exchanged and the money given. Then this other man scurried away. He wasn't the type with whom Cole and his sidekicks would associate unless they were up to something.'

'How you mean?' pressed Cap.

'Well, he was a weedy, shifty individual, shabbily dressed in a frock-coat.'

Cap nodded his understanding. 'Who'd you figure he was?'

'Don't know, and I didn't get a chance to follow him. I'd have been seen by Dutch. Dutch returned to the saloon and all three were still there when I left.'

'Good work, Rusty.'

'What do we do now?'

'If we can get a line on this weedy individual we might get a lead, but maybe we can't do that until tomorrow. Meantime I reckon when it's dark we can move into town and keep our eyes on Cole's sidekicks.'

By the time they had eaten the light was fading fast.

'We'll leave the horses short of the saloon. I'll wait with them while you check it out,' said Cap as they neared the first houses in Mather.

There were a few people about when they

slipped from the saddles, and Rusty handed his reins to Cap. He moved away without a word and strolled casually to the saloon. Two men passed him and pushed the batwings open. Rusty slowed and hesitated momentarily when he reached the first window. A quick glance told him nothing except that the saloon was doing a good trade. He moved on. The second window gave him a better view, and he thought he saw Pecos at the bar but he needed to confirm it. When he reached the batwings he stopped and looked over them into the room. Pecos. Further along the bar, Jake and Dutch. He turned away quickly. He had seen all he wanted to. He crossed the street and walked back to Cap.

'They're still there,' he informed Cap.

'Good. I figure they won't be leaving town tonight. But we'll hang around for a while, make sure.'

'Maybe they're waiting here for Cole,' suggested Rusty.

'All the better if they are,' said Cap.

'You figure on taking 'em here?'

'I'll take 'em anywhere as soon as I know why they tried to hang me.'

'They're sure going to get the pants scared off them when they see you,' chuckled Rusty.

Cap was beginning to think it was time they called off their vigil when the three men emerged from the saloon. Dutch and Pecos were supporting Jake, while two saloon girls, carrying bottles, tagged along. With raucous shouts and laughter the group weaved its way across the street to the hotel.

'I reckon we can forget them for the night,' commented Cap, and he started to unfasten the reins from the hitching rail.

'Sure,' agreed Rusty. 'But what about the morning? How about me taking a room so's I can keep tabs on them?'

'Good idea,' agreed Cap. 'And it gives me an idea. Maybe we can get Jake, in his state, to talk. You get your room, locate them and unlock the door to the fire escape.'

The two men parted. Rusty took his horse

to the livery stable and then found himself a room at the hotel. He was on the same floor as the three men he was watching, and the noise coming from two of the rooms indicated that the middle one was possibly that being used by Jake. He unlocked the door at the end of the dimly lit passage and then waited in his room with the door slightly ajar.

A few minutes later he felt the presence of someone in the corridor rather than heard him, Cap had made his entry so silently.

Rusty eased the door open, saw Cap and made his presence known. Cap stepped quickly into the room.

'I figure Jake is in the one opposite mine,' said Rusty quietly.

Cap nodded. 'The others on either side by the noise.'

'What you reckon doing?' queried Rusty.

'Scare the pants off Jake like you said I would,' grinned Cap. 'Maybe learn something if he's not too drunk. See if the corridor's clear.'

Rusty eased the door ajar and peered through the gap. No sound except from two rooms on the opposite side of the corridor. No one in his range of vision. He opened the door wider and looked round it. Nobody. He opened the door wide, stepped outside and immediately Cap was with him.

One step took him to the door opposite. He grasped the knob firmly, eased it round and pushed the door open slowly. Heavy, regular breathing indicated someone asleep. Cap pushed the door wider while Rusty, with Colt in his hand, watched the corridor. As soon as Cap was inside, Rusty was beside him with the door closed. A lamp, turned low, gave sufficient light to reveal a fully dressed Jake sprawled across the bed.

'Don't reckon you'll get much sense out of him,' whispered Rusty close to Cap's ear.

Cap nodded. He was inclined to agree with Rusty, but he'd try.

'Get behind him, Rusty.'

Rusty moved quietly round the bed and, knowing instinctively what Cap wanted of him, he turned his Colt so he held it by the barrel. If the situation arose, Jake would not know what hit him.

Cap removed one bullet from the chamber in his Colt. He moved the table and lamp and arranged them so that the light lit his face and intensified the darkness of the room. He stared at Jake and indicated to Rusty to prod him.

Jake moaned. Rusty prodded him again. Jake stirred and struggled to raise himself on one elbow.

'Why did you hang me?' Cap made his tone quiet yet deep.

Jake stiffened.

'Why did you hang me?' Cap's voice became more penetrating.

Jake jerked. His head came round. His eyes widened with fright when he saw Cap's head as if it was disembodied and suspended in space. He scrambled back on the bed and cowered, shaking with fright as the head swayed slightly from side to side.

'Why?' The word was drawn out in a long

whisper from Cap.

'We was told to.' Jake's voice shook with fright.

'Who told you?'

'Cole.'

'Who told him?'

'I dunno.'

'Who?'

Jake began to shake even more, and when he spoke his words were even more slurred, the result of drink and fear.

'Honest, I dunno. Cole didn't tell us.'

'Why?'

Jake shook his head.

'Who did Dutch meet in the alley?'

Jake continued shaking his head. His body trembled more and more. Cap reckoned he would get no more information out of Jake even if he knew anything.

Cap raised his Colt slowly and as it came into the range of the light and pointed at him Jake's fear widened in his eyes. He cringed as if it would help him escape from the weapon. His lips voiced a soundless scream.

Cap squeezed the trigger. As the hammer struck an empty chamber Jake fainted.

Cap quickly set the table and lamp as they had been when they entered the room. He and Rusty crossed the corridor, and once in Rusty's room they relaxed and grins broadened their faces.

'You sure scared him,' chuckled Rusty.

'I'd hoped he'd tell me more.'

'Do you figure he really didn't know anything else?'

'I reckon so. I think he was so scared stiff he'd have told me if he'd known.'

'So Cole's the key to your hanging party.'

'Looks like it.'

'And that meeting in the alley which I witnessed probably has nothing to do with it.'

'Maybe, maybe not. Could be just Dutch's affair. But we'll not ignore it. You stay here the night. See what the reactions are when Jake wakes up, and in the morning see if you can get a lead on the man Dutch met in the alley.'

Rusty agreed. After he had checked the corridor, Cap left the hotel by the fire escape, and Rusty relocked the door.

7

A noise in the corridor brought Rusty instantly awake. As he slipped out of bed he figured, from the light coming through the window, that it was shortly after dawn. With the door ajar he saw the two girls go to the stairs. A few moments later, from his window, he saw them cross the street to the saloon.

Rusty figured there could be action from the other side of the corridor any time, so he dressed and waited. Half an hour passed before he heard a screech, a door crash open and a voice yelling, 'Dutch! Pecos!'

Another door slammed open and the cry of 'Dutch! Dutch!' burst out.

From the gap in his door, Rusty saw Pecos race to Dutch's room. 'What the hell's going on?' he called.

'Stop jabbering, Jake! You mad or something?' Rusty heard Dutch say harshly.

'I ain't mad. It was his head!'

'What's he talking about?' rasped Pecos.

'I saw him. I did, Pecos, I did.' Jake's words came fast. 'His head. It was there in my room.'

'You drank too much,' snapped Dutch.

'Maybe, but Millet was there. He spoke to me.'

'Hell, talk sense,' rapped Pecos. 'We hung him. You've had nightmares.'

'So, it was his ghost. But it's after us. Revenge for what we did.'

'Ghosts can't do such things,' said Dutch derisively.

'This one can. It shot me.'

'Shot you?' Dutch and Pecos laughed. 'So you're dead.'

'He pointed a gun at me and squeezed the trigger.'

'Then what?'

'I don't remember any more.'

'Exactly. A nightmare. Then you woke up.' Dutch tried to dismiss the matter.

'Did you meet someone in the alley?' insisted Jake.

'Now what you talking about?' A little sharpness had come to Dutch's voice.

'His head wanted to know who you had met in the alley.'

'What else did he say?' asked Dutch, directing attention away from that point, though puzzled by it.

'Asked me who told us to hang him?'

'What did you tell him?'

'Cole, that's all I could. You know as well as me that Cole never told us who paid us.'

'Were you in the alley, Dutch?' asked Pecos.

There was a slight hesitation before Dutch spoke. 'Yeah. I was doing a job for Cole.'

'Hi, there ain't a double-cross–'

'Hell, no,' broke in Dutch harshly.

'We'll get the rest of the cash?' There was still doubt in Pecos's voice.

'Sure. Cole was paid so much in cash. The rest was in two notes, one on the bank in White Hills, the other on the bank here.

Cole asked me to do some checking before he arrived. Said the fewer who knew about it the better. You know Cole. So we wait until he comes.'

'Right.' Pecos seemed satisfied. 'Now there's one thing which puzzles me. If Jake saw Cap Millet–'

'I did!' Jake cut in.

'Then I reckon it was Millet, alive.'

'Why do you figure that?' queried Dutch.

'He knew about your meeting in the alley and that was after we hung him. I reckon ghosts don't know about happenings after the death of the person whose ghost they are.'

'But we hung him,' insisted Dutch.

'We didn't make sure that he was dead,' Pecos pointed out.

'That's right, we didn't.' Jake lent weight to Pecos's statement. 'I mentioned it to Cole but he said we should keep riding, that there was no way Millet could escape, but it seems he did.'

'It still takes some swallowing,' said

Dutch. 'If he is alive, how'd he know where to find us?'

'That has me puzzled,' agreed Pecos, 'but let's not bother about that. If he's around we'll be ready for him. Let's check the rest of the rooms.'

Rusty did not want them bursting in on him so he stepped into the corridor as the three men, with Colts drawn, hurried out of Dutch's room.

'Say, you fellas are–' Rusty feigned surprise at the sight of Dutch, Jake and Pecos.

They showed equal surprise. 'Rusty! What the hell are you doing here?'

'Needed to see a man about some horses,' said Rusty, hoping they were too preoccupied with their own thoughts to pry into his answer. 'You sure are making one hell of a din. What's going on?'

'When did you get in, Rusty?' asked Dutch.

'Late last night. Why?'

'See anyone else?'

'No. Heard some noise coming from those two rooms. Someone was having a good time.' He grinned.

'What about the middle one. Hear anything there?'

'Just heavy breathing as if someone was in a sound sleep.'

Dutch grunted. 'See or hear anyone else around at any time during the night?'

'No. When I hit the sack I slept until you fellas woke me.' He glanced at each one in turn. 'Anything wrong?'

'No, not really,' replied Dutch. 'Jake reckoned there was someone in his room during the night. We're searching to satisfy him. Pecos and I reckon he'd had too much to drink.' He gave a knowing laugh and winked at Rusty.

'I see,' grinned Rusty. 'Well, I'll leave you to it.' Rusty stepped past them and went down the stairs. He heard doors being opened and shut, and smiled to himself.

Once he had got his horse from the livery stable he took precautions by leaving the town in the opposite direction to the one he wanted. He saw no reason to be followed, but he knew where Cole and his sidekicks were concerned he could not be too cautious.

Once he was certain that he was not being trailed he rode swiftly to Cap and acquainted him of what had happened.

'You reckon they figure I'm alive?' asked Cap when Rusty had finished his story.

'Yeah. I think your knowledge of the meeting in the alley finally convinced Dutch and Pecos that there was more to this than Jake's over-drinking.'

'No matter,' said Cap with a shrug of his shoulders. 'It's given us a pointer that they are up to something. It might be connected with their attempt to hang me.'

'What happens now?' asked Rusty.

'We know they're going to wait here for Cole. According to my reckoning that should be the day after tomorrow. So we sit tight. Now they know you're here you'd better be seen around town, so you keep your hotel room. See if you can get a lead on that hombre Dutch met in the alley.'

'And you?'

'Reckon there ain't much to do but wait Cole's arrival.'

'You going to take 'em then?'

'I want to know why they tried to hang me before I have that pleasure.'

Four hours later, when Rusty returned, he brought the information that Dutch, Pecos and Jake were spending their time in the saloon and that the man whom Dutch had met in the alley worked as a clerk in the bank.

'Interesting,' mused Cap. 'Dutch paying for information?'

'You mean about the bank's security?' queried Rusty.

'Could be. Maybe they're planning a robbery. Do you know if that's their type of crime?'

'Ain't done anything like that. Robbery? Not them. Hired guns is their game.'

'Then why a secret contact with a bank clerk in Mather?' puzzled Cap.

8

When Cole rode into Mather he made straight for the hotel and was given the room next to Dutch's which had been previously booked for him by his sidekick.

A few minutes later, a hotel clerk, anxious not to displease the new arrival, panted a message to Dutch in the saloon. On a signal from Dutch three glasses were drained and three men hurried from the saloon.

This incident had been carefully observed by Rusty, supposedly whiling away his time over a beer at a table in one corner of the room. The departure of the three men had been so quick after the clerk had spoken to Dutch that Rusty reckoned Cole must have arrived in town. He finished his drink and strolled casually from the saloon. Pausing on the sidewalk he noted the dust-covered horse hitched to the rail in front of the hotel and figured that he was right in his supposition about Cole.

He hesitated, trying to decide what to do. He knew that he should inform Cap as arranged, but he wondered if he could gain any more information if he returned to the hotel.

Stepping off the sidewalk he headed for the livery stable. He glanced at the hotel and wondered what was going on in one of its rooms on the first floor. He changed direction, and a few moments later was quietly climbing the stairs in the hotel, listening intently for any noise in the corridor above.

Reaching the top step, he hesitated. No sound. He edged on to the corridor, and six quick steps took him to the door of his room. He paused. The buzz of voices came from the room next to Dutch's. He glanced towards the top of the stairs. All was quiet below. Inching nearer the door he strained to try to hear what was being said behind the closed door, but it was no use. He stepped quickly to his own door and moved into the room leaving the door ajar. Maybe if he couldn't overhear anything he could pick up something from their actions and be able to report something more positive to Cap. Rusty waited.

When the three men entered Cole's room greetings were exchanged with Pecos adding, 'Got the money, Cole?'

'From White Hills. Still have to visit the bank here. Will do that in a few minutes.'

'Good,' grinned Jake. 'Then we can sure live it up.'

'Not so fast,' said Cole. 'We're playing for bigger stakes.'

'What you getting at?' asked Pecos with a look which matched the surprised curiosity on the faces of his two companions.

'All in good time,' replied Cole.' I gained some information in White Hills which has got to be followed up, but first I want to know what Dutch found out.' He glanced at the man who chewed on a cheroot.

'Fletcher opened an account here in 1865

with a large sum of money,' reported Dutch.

Cole grinned. 'Exactly what happened in White Hills.' There was a touch of excitement in his voice. 'And I learned more. The money in White Hills was transferred from an account in Claystone and that account was left with an identical sum.'

'Then Fletcher sure had some cash in 1865,' said Dutch.

'Yeah. But I can also tell you he bought land at the same time.'

'What you getting at?' queried Jake.

'All in good time,' grinned Cole with some satisfaction. 'I was curious when Fletcher gave us notes to draw on two banks and paid us cash which he must have obtained from a bank nearer to his ranch, that must have been in Claystone. I figured it was worth looking into. Well, it looks as though it's going to prove worthwhile.'

'How?' questioned Jake.

'Later,' returned Cole. 'I've some more checking to do on Fletcher. It'll take me away for a couple of days, but when I'm

back I reckon Fletcher is in for a big shock.'
He glanced sharply at his three sidekicks. 'I
got a surprise when I rode into Durango on
my way here. Cap Millet didn't die. He'd
been in Durango making enquiries about
us. Ed and Hal got the drop on him but
somehow with the aid of Rusty he got away.
Still that needn't worry us, they won't know
where we are and they don't know of our
connection with Fletcher.'

'Rusty!' Dutch gasped. 'So that's why he's
here.'

'Rusty, here?' Cole stared in amazement at
Dutch.

'Yeah, and Millet!' burst in Jake. 'He was
in my room.'

'What!' Cole's eyes widened with impact
of the news.

Dutch quickly explained what had happened.

As he listened Cole's mind was dealing
coolly with the facts. 'I reckon when we
collected our horses from Rusty we must
have said something which gave him a clue

as to where we were heading. Did he say what he was doing here?'

'Dealing in some horses.'

'A blind. He's the eyes for Cap Millet while he lies low.'

'Seen Rusty today?'

'No. Heard him in his room when we went out.'

'He's staying here in the hotel?' Cole was surprised, but even as he showed it he guessed there was no reason for Rusty not to stay here. He would never surmise that he would be rumbled through the incident in Durango.

'Right opposite.'

'Let's see if he's there now. I figure he can tell us where Cap is and we can finish a job we started with a hanging-tree.' The cruel streak in Cole's eyes glowed as he drew his Colt.

He opened the door of his room slightly and peered through the gap. All was quiet on the corridor. He noted that Rusty's door was ajar. He eased his door shut and turned to his sidekicks. 'I reckon he's in. We'll make it fast to his room.' They nodded.

Dutch spat out his unlit cheroot and drew his gun. Pecos did likewise, and Jake ran his finger down the blade of his knife anticipating the pleasure of making Rusty talk.

Suddenly Cole jerked the door open and the four men swept into Rusty's room. Rusty did not have time to move away from the door and the force of the entry sent him staggering backwards to tumble on to the bed. Quick to recover from his surprise, he saw it was useless to retaliate, for he stared at three Colts and a knife.

'What the hell's going on?' he protested.

'You tell us,' rapped Cole as he bent forward and jerked Rusty's Colt out of its holster. He glanced at Dutch and Pecos, and on the slight nod of his head they holstered their weapons, grabbed Rusty and dragged him roughly from the bed.

Cole buried his fist hard into Rusty's stomach. He doubled up with a gasp of pain, but Dutch and Pecos jerked him

111

upright. Cole hit him hard in the stomach again bringing a cry from the older man's lips as hot pain seared through his body.

Cole leered at him. 'That's just a sample of what you'll get if you don't talk.'

'I don't know what you want.' Rusty's words came in gasps as he tried to draw breath to ease the pain.

'Information. You helped Cap Millet in Durango. Where is he?'

Rusty's mind raced. So that was it. Cole must have come from Durango. Just their luck to be rumbled by a chance visit.

'I don't know what you're talking about,' Rusty spat.

Cole's eyes clouded with anger. He struck Rusty hard across the mouth, drawing blood from one corner. 'Liar. You talk and save yourself a lot of pain.' He glared close at Rusty's face. ''Cos you can have it.'

Rusty glared silently at Cole. Cole slapped him hard across the face with a series of blows which cut his left cheek and brought a swelling to his right eye.

'Talk,' snarled Cole. 'Where's Millet?'

Rusty shook his head. 'Don't know. We parted outside of Durango.' The words came as hurt whispers between swelling lips.

'Liar. Millet was in Jake's room and I figure you told him where Jake was. Millet couldn't have picked the only room where there wasn't a girl unless he'd been tipped off. You were the informer. So where is he?' To add force to his question Cole drove his fist into Rusty's stomach again.

A cry of pain burst on the wind driven out of the beaten man. Rusty gasped for breath. His knees buckled, but he was held in vice-like grips on either side of him.

'Don't be a fool,' rasped Cole. 'Talk and save yourself any more hurt.'

Rusty, his mind reeling, automatically shook his head. Pain exploded inside him again with the next blow. He felt himself falling. Instinctively his hands came out to save himself. His knees hit the floor. He pitched forward. His arms supported him, but only momentarily, for a blow pounded

the middle of his back sending him sprawling.

He winced as boots were driven into his
side. His mind, wavering on the edge of unconsciousness, screamed for the pain to
end. Dimly he was aware of voices.

'Hold it. We don't want him passing out.'

'Let me, I know a way to make him talk.'

'Get that jug of water.'

Rusty started with the sudden impact of
the cold water. His mind cleared a little so
that he was more conscious of the hurt
which ripped through his body. More cold
water sloshed over his head. Then he felt
hands grasp both his arms and drag him to
his feet.

'Your last chance,' hissed Cole, 'or I turn
Jake on you. Where's Millet?'

Rusty, water dripping from his lank hair,
glared with an undeniable hatred at Cole
from eyes which were closing rapidly. Blood
ran down his cheek and from his mouth,
and as he shook his head he spat blood at
Cole.

Anger flared in Cole. In one movement his Colt was out of its holster and raised to strike Rusty, but he stopped himself. Rusty had to talk and it had to be now. He lowered his arm slowly and slipped the gun back into its holster. He wiped his sleeve across his face and said, 'Jake.'

Jake's face broke into an evil leer filled with a sadistic pleasure at the thought of what he was to do.

He glanced at Dutch and Pecos. 'Chair and table,' he instructed.

The two men forced Rusty on to the chair beside the table and held him firm by the arms. Jake sat down on a chair opposite Rusty.

'You going to co-operate?' he asked with a casualness which bore a threat of terrible things if Rusty refused.

'Go to hell!' rapped Rusty.

Jake's eyes darkened. He glanced up at Dutch. 'Right hand.'

Dutch jerked Rusty's right hand on to the table, and before he could offer any resistance Dutch's weight had spread his fingers out fan-shaped facing Jake. Jake held his knife-point upwards in front of Rusty and felt the sharpness of the point while he grinned sadistically at his victim.

'Talk?' hissed Cole close to Rusty's ear. Rusty made no reply. 'It will hurt like hell when Jake works on your nails.'

The shock of knowing what was going to happen cleared Rusty's mind as it was meant to do. Cole wanted him fully aware so that the pain would be more intense and induce a breakdown of Rusty's resistance.

Rusty remained silent.

Cole glanced at Jake and nodded.

Jake took hold of Rusty's forefinger. Slowly and deliberately he inserted the point of the knife between the nail and the skin.

Pain shot through Rusty. He winced, stifling the cry which it brought.

Jake pushed. The point went further, tearing the skin from the nail. Rusty gulped, bit his swollen lips, but then as he felt the knife dragged slowly sideways he could no longer hold back the scream.

The pressure stopped. The pain stayed.

'Want to talk now?' The question penetrated Rusty's bemused brain.

He swallowed hard. Then the knife cut sideways again. Rusty stiffened trying to stifle his cry. Sweat broke out on his forehead and his whole body was suddenly wrapped in the dampness of fear.

'We'll leave that one for a moment,' he heard a voice saying smoothly. 'We'll try the next one.'

Rusty struggled to move his hand, but it was useless against Dutch's pressure. He felt the blade pierce the skin below the nail of his longest finger. This time Jake did not exert a gentle pressure but made a quick penetration.

Rusty screamed with the sudden agony.

'I can make it slow, I can make it fast.' Jake added emphasis to his words by moving the knife sideways. 'But I can go on doing it. And when I've loosened them we can have a great time pulling them off.' Jake's voice was silky, emphasising the torture which faced Rusty. So that his victim was left in no doubt, Jake thrust the knife deeper.

Rusty shook. He writhed on his chair.

'Where's Millet?' asked Cole, his voice in Rusty's mind as sharp as the knife to which Jake gave an extra twist.

Rusty nodded vigorously. He had to stop the excruciating pain. He felt the knife withdrawn.

'Where?' Cole demanded.

'West trail. Group of rocks about two miles out of town.' The words staggered between his bloody lips. He felt the grip on his arms relax and disappear. A blow pounded the side of his head, exploding his mind into blackness.

9

Cap Millet was up early, cleared his camp, made his horse ready to ride at a moment's notice, and then settled down to watch. He believed in being prepared. Today was the day when Cole should be joining his side-kicks in Mather. When he did, Rusty would inform him and they would be ready if the four men moved on. If not, he had lost nothing.

The morning dragged on into the early afternoon. Once again, as he had frequently done throughout the day, Cap trained his spyglass on the edge of Mather where the west trail left the town. No Rusty. There was no knowing what time of day Cole was arriving. Maybe there had been a change in his plan, but at least his sidekicks were still there.

Cap stiffened. A rider. Rusty? Three more

were close behind, so it couldn't be Rusty. Cap relaxed and eased himself against the huge rock which gave him protection from the direct heat of the sun.

He glanced casually in the direction of town. The four riders shimmered ghost-like in the heat-haze thrown up from the ground. They were using the west trail.

Cap waited. A few minutes later he put his spyglass to his eye and trained it on the edge of town. Still no sign of Rusty. He moved his gaze slowly along the west trail to the four riders. Now he was able to combat the haze and draw them into better focus.

Suddenly every nerve in Cap's body went taut. Pecos! He moved his sight to each of the other riders in quick succession. Dutch! Jake! And Cole!

Cole was here. He had contacted his side-kicks. Why hadn't Rusty informed him? Had Rusty been rumbled? A cold feeling of doom swept over Cap. What had happened to that likeable stableman who had teamed up with him?

While watching the four men Cap was trying to make up his mind on his next move. He must find out what had happened to Rusty but that might mean losing contact with Cole. They would pass close to him as they rode the west trail and he was in an ideal position to follow. But even as he watched his immediate move was decided for him.

He saw Cole signal to his sidekicks, and in response they split the direction of their ride and quickened their pace, the two outside men riding faster than the others. They were aiming to cover his hide-out from all sides!

The realisation stunned Cap. They knew where he was! And that could mean only one thing, Rusty had been made to talk. Worry for his friend, anger at what might have happened and the need to survive rode equally in Cap's mind. He could stand and fight, pick them off one by one. He had the advantage. He would get his revenge, but dead men would not give him the answers he wanted.

Cap raced to his horse and leaped into the

saddle. As he pulled the animal round he slammed his spyglass into its leather pouch hanging from his saddlehorn. He stabbed the animal into a gallop, weaved through the rocks and burst into the open at a dead run.

His sudden appearance was a signal for the four riders to urge their horses in pursuit. The crash of gunfire broke above the thunder of pounding hooves. Bullets whined harmlessly, and the pursuers gave up any more attempts to unseat Cap. They would wait until they were nearer, more certain to make a hit. They concentrated on closing the distance while Cap was equally determined that they shouldn't.

Anxiously, Cap glanced over his shoulder. He was holding the gap between himself and his pursuers. He needed to reach the hill country three miles away without them gaining. His horse responded to his call for greater effort.

Ground flew beneath the earth-tearing hooves. Cap put his animal at the slope knowing that once over the rise he would be hidden from the eyes of his pursuers for a brief time. It was a chance he must seize.

His horse slowed. Cole and his sidekicks gained a few yards, then they were starting up the slope. Millet, his horse breathing heavily with the exertion, reached the summit. Immediately it lengthened its stride into a more measured beat. Cap's eyes searched the hilly landscape and hit upon a valley which cut away to his left. He eased his horse in its direction, and the animal, seeming to sense a possible escape, quickened its pace.

But it was not sufficient. Cap was still in sight when Cole broke the rise, and without hesitation turned in pursuit.

Cap thundered into the valley and kept his horse running, fully aware that he must not get trapped here for there was nothing to give him any cover. The valley started to narrow, its sides steepening. Ahead they would be impossible to climb, so Cap turned his horse to the right and urged the animal up the slope before it became too steep.

Earth and stones, loosened by the cutting

hooves, rolled back down the hillside as the horse struggled upwards.

With a yell of triumph Cole brought his horse to a halt at the bottom of the slope. He drew his rifle from its scabbard, raised it to his shoulder and squeezed the trigger. But he had been too anxious, too eager to stop Cap escaping, and in his haste had not drawn an accurate line on his target. The bullet struck the earth to Cap's right. Anger now destroyed his aim as he loosed off two more shots. Then Cap was out of range again. Cole cursed and, as his sidekicks pulled up alongside him, he kicked his horse forward and yelled to them to get after Cap.

When he reached the top of the slope, Cap found himself on a ridge with a steep drop in front of them. He hesitated momentarily while he quickly surveyed the landscape for a means of escape.

He turned his horse to his left and followed the ridge which swung right and dropped towards an outcrop of rocks covering a considerable area before giving way to two rock-strewn valleys. Cap saw a chance. If he could lose himself in the outcrop his pursuers would not know whether he had stopped or taken to one of the two valleys. But he must gain the cover before one of the riders behind him reached the ridge. He called to his horse, his voice urging. The animal stretched its stride. Earth flew.

Cap leaned low in the saddle, his eyes fixed on the outcrop. He started, taken aback by something he had failed to notice. The ridge narrowed for about a hundred yards with a sharp drop on either side. Automatically he went to check the horse, but resisted the temptation. He kept the pace. He could gain precious time. The horse thundered on. Then animal and rider were upon it. Cap was aware of steep inclines flashing past him. One false step and he would be doomed, but the horse never faltered. The ridge widened and, as if marking its success, the horse carried Cap to the rocky cover with a final surge.

Cap turned the animal behind the first

outcrop and brought it to a halt. He swung out of the saddle on to the rock and scrambled up its smooth slope to view the ridge he had just left. No one! They had not reached the ridge! He had beaten them!

Cap drew a deep breath of relief, turned and slithered down the rock to his horse. The animal was still heaving after its exertion, and its sweating body steamed. Cap swung into the saddle and guided his mount between the rocks until he came to an area of flat hard ground. His trail would disappear here, a place from which he could have taken any number of directions. Cap sized up the position quickly and found what he was looking for a short distance to his right.

He rode to the slit in the rock-face and slipped from the saddle. He led the horse into the cutting which curved to the left and spiralled upwards. The ground flattened and widened into a space with a convenient overhang below which he could leave his horse with safety. He slipped his rifle from its leather and continued up the twisting path until it gave out on a huge flat area of rock which sloped gently upwards to his right.

Cap climbed the slope quickly and found, as he had suspected, that he was in a position which overlooked the large expanse of rock area where he had been able to lose his trail. He was above the slit in the rock which had given him access to this position. If by any freak chance Cole and his sidekicks decided to search that slit, he could defend himself with ease.

Cap listened intently. There was no sound of galloping horses. In its place voices called at each other. Although he could not make out the words he guessed that his pursuers had not had the nerve to cross the narrowest part of the ridge at full gallop. As if to verify his conclusion the sound of horses breaking into a gallop reached his ears a few minutes later. He heard them slow at the outcrop of rocks.

He flattened himself so that he could just peer over the edge of the rock on which he lay. He would see without being seen.

'Trail's here.'

'We'll get the bastard.'

The voices came from beyond the tumble of rocks.

'Hell.'

'What's wrong?'

'Trail's gone.'

The voices were closer.

'Damn this rock.'

'Lost it.'

'No chance of picking it up now.'

'He could have ridden in any direction.'

The four men, leading their horses, appeared on the vast expanse of rock.

'Could be anywhere around here.'

'Aye, or away down one of those two valleys we saw as we came off the ridge.'

'Pecos, stay here with the horses. We'll cast around, see if we can pick up a clue.' Cole issued the order.

Pecos took the reins from the others who then began their search.

Cap kept close watch on them all. He

tensed as Dutch moved closer to the rock on which he was hiding.

For one moment he thought the man below was going to investigate the slit in the rock, but Dutch turned away and directed his attention elsewhere.

After minutes Cole called a halt. 'Its useless,' he shouted. 'No sign of a trail and we can't search every cleft.'

'I reckon he'd keep riding,' said Pecos as the others joined him.

'More than likely,' agreed Cole. 'He could be miles away by now.'

'Are we forgetting him?' asked Jake.

'He ain't a man to forget,' rapped Cole. 'But if he's foolish enough to come back we'll be ready.'

'Maybe he's seen sense and cleared off for good now he realises that we know he's still alive.'

'He sure won't want that rope again and he knows he'll get it if he does return.'

'What now, Cole?'

'We'll continue with our plans. I'm going

to Pincher Creek. See you in Durango in three days and then, if my figuring is correct, we'll make a big killing.'

'Don't run out on us, Cole,' said Dutch, a touch of ice to his voice.

'You suspicious?' rapped Cole testily.

'No. Cautious,' returned Dutch.

'Hell, I ain't thinking of running out on you. If I was I wouldn't have come to Mather. I could need the backing of three good guns when the time comes, so I'll be back.'

Dutch nodded.

The four men swung into the saddles and rode away.

Cap remained where he was until long after they had gone.

10

Cap could hardly believe his luck. He still had a lead on the four would-be hangmen, though he knew he would have to employ the utmost caution when he picked up their trail again, especially as it would be in the vicinity of Durango.

He wished he had been able to follow Cole. Maybe Cole's destination would have given him a clue to the 'big killing' Cole had talked about. And in turn that may have presented a lead about the hanging. But whatever the chances offered by trailing Cole he must forgo them. The important thing now was to find out about Rusty and whether there was a murder as well as an attempted hanging to revenge. Cap was eager to do so as soon as possible, but he curbed his impatience. It would be fatal to ride too soon. Cole and his sidekicks must get no hint that they had left him behind.

Once he did move, Cap lost no time in reaching Mather. When he saw the knot of people gathered outside the hotel a coldness gripped him. Rusty!

The sound of the galloping horse drew their attention. Heads turned to see who rode at such a pace. When the rider slid his horse to a halt outside the hotel and was out of the saddle before it stopped they knew instinctively that the stranger had something to do with the trouble inside the hotel. They moved out of his way as he leaped on to the sidewalk and strode into the building.

A few people spoke in low tones in the lobby.

'Rusty Parks?' asked Cap sharply.

'Room five, first floor.' Cap never knew who answered him, but he was at the stairs, mounting them quickly.

He turned on to the corridor and saw the doorway of room five was filled by a broad back. Cap grabbed the man by the shoulder and pulled him backwards. The man, caught unawares, staggered.

'What the—' he gasped.

'Sorry, sheriff,' apologised Cap quickly when he saw the badge pinned to the shirt. 'Rusty's a friend of mine.'

'Who're you?' demanded the lawman.

'Cap Millet,' replied Cap. 'What has happened?'

'He's been badly beaten up. Doc's with him now.'

Cap spun round and pushed into the room.

Rusty was on the bed. Conscious. An elderly man in his shirt-sleeves bent over him. He glanced at Cap when Cap appeared at his side, then ignored him to get on with his task of tending to the ugly wounds.

'Rusty, it's Cap,' said Cap quietly, as he leaned forward.

''I'm sorry,' croaked Rusty, and then winced with the effort of moving his mouth.

'Don't talk,' urged Cap. 'I'm all right.' He sensed the relief that his arrival had brought to his friend. He knew that Rusty must have been worried because he had given Cap's position away to Cole. 'Important thing is for you to get better. He'll be all right, won't he, Doc?'

'It will take time, but he'll mend. He's taken a nasty beating. Lucky to be alive,' replied the doctor without interrupting his task. 'Seen his fingers?'

Cap glanced down at the hands laid on top of the sheet and winced when he saw nails hanging loose on torn flesh.

'Hell! I'm sorry you suffered because of me, old friend. Doc, take care of him until I get back. See he has the best of everything.'

'Cap, don't–' Rusty made an effort to speak, but Cap halted him.

'Must, Rusty, I have a lead.'

Rusty moved his head in some sort of nod. 'Be careful.' The whisper reached Cap.

'I will. I'll be back,' he reassured.

Cap turned to the door.

As the sheriff moved, he said, 'I'd like a word with you before you leave.'

'Make it quick, sheriff,' replied Cap. 'I want the bastards who did that to Rusty.'

'You know them?'

Cap told the sheriff only what he wanted him to know, but it was sufficient to satisfy.

'See here, Millet,' said the sheriff when Cap had finished. 'I know how you feel but don't go taking the law into your own hands.'

'Where those bastards are heading there is no law,' rapped Cap. 'Care to try and take them in Durango?'

'Durango! You're sure right, there ain't any law there. It's outside my jurisdiction anyway. My hands are tied, so good luck to you.'

'Thanks, sheriff,' said Cap. 'Don't let Rusty leave town. He might try something foolish. I hope I'll be back in a week.' Cap stepped past the sheriff then paused. 'How come no one stopped them. Rusty must have yelled?'

'Hotel clerk heard the screams, came up to investigate. When he saw what was happening he threatened to get the law but he was told he'd get the same if he did. In case anybody else was drawn by Rusty's shouts they told the clerk to go back downstairs and stop anybody nosing. In any case I was out of town.'

Cap grunted and left. When he reached the street he rode his horse to the livery stable and hired a fresh animal.

Once his saddle and belongings had been transferred to the best mount the stableman had to offer, Cap left Mather at a quick pace.

He knew when Cole would show in Durango. Cole was the key, only he knew who had hired him to do the hanging, and only he knew what the future plans were. So Cole was his prime target; from him he would get all the answers. He'd make the others pay for what they did to Rusty, and he needn't wait for Cole's return to do that. Cap rode hard to try to re-establish contact before dark.

He was beginning to think that he had failed and that he had better be making camp when a sudden flare, splitting the darkness, some distance ahead and to his right, caused him to pull his horse to a halt. A flame. The glow went out. Cap waited. It came again, then subsided to a flickering gleam.

Someone had made a fire. Someone making camp for the night? Cole and his sidekicks? Maybe Cole had already left them. Maybe it was a stranger. Cap had to find out.

He put his horse into a walking pace and rode until he figured it was no longer safe to do so. He slipped from the saddle and walked with his animal until he found a low bush to which he could hitch it. Cap moved carefully towards the glow and stopped when he could see that it was close to an overhang of rock with the grassland giving way to an area of scrubland of low bushes as it approached the rock. He should be able to get close to the camp without betraying his presence and have cover from which he could study it.

He twisted his way stealthily between the bushes until he deemed it wisest to crawl. He paused every now and then to survey the ground ahead, and eventually made out three figures sitting around the fire. The mumble of conversation reached him. He inched forward carefully, manoeuvring into a position so that he could identify the three men.

Pecos, Dutch, and Jake! Cap felt the glow of satisfaction at making contact again. Cole had already left them, but Cap knew when he could pick up his trail again. Cap eased himself into a more comfortable position.

The urge to avenge Rusty was strong. He could easily pick these men off before they knew what was happening. But he didn't want it that way. They must know Rusty was being avenged, that they were being made to pay for what they did to the stableman. Cap was prepared to wait and seize any opportunity which was presented. He watched and listened.

'What do you figure Cole's up to?' It was

Jake's voice.

'Does it matter?' said Dutch. 'He said we'd make a big killing and that'll suit me without asking any questions.'

'Wonder if it's anything to do with Millet?' mused Jake.

'Better if you wondered where he is,' put in Pecos.

'I reckon he was still high-tailin' it even though we lost his trail,' said Jake. 'He wouldn't want the hanging rope again.'

'He could have doubled back to check on Rusty,' said Pecos.

'Cole didn't figure that way,' said Dutch.

'I know, but I ain't so sure,' said Pecos. 'He's a smart operator. Look how he got into Jake's room.'

'With Rusty's help,' Dutch pointed out.

'Sure. That's why I think he might have gone back to Mather. Doesn't strike me as being the type who'd desert someone who had helped him.'

'Say, if you feel that way why don't you go back to Mather and check?' said Jake.

'Might not be a bad idea,' said Pecos. 'I sure feel uneasy not knowing where he is.'

'But he can't know where we are or that we're heading for Durango,' Dutch pointed out.

'Maybe not. But I don't think he's going to let up on that hanging so easily. Remember he must have got a lead on us through Durango to be teamed up with Rusty. He may figure on trying Durango again,' said Pecos.

'Quit going on about it, Pecos. You'll have us uneasy, like you,' snapped Dutch.

'You go back,' said Jake. 'You've time before Cole shows up in Durango. And if you get Millet on the end of a gun be sure you don't miss.'

The subject was dropped and desultory conversation continued for half an hour before Cap saw the three men settle down for the night.

He slid away quietly and returned to his horse and made his own sleeping-place. Maybe tomorrow would present him with an opportunity he wanted. He must be awake early, before the men he watched were on the move.

The first light was breaking the eastern horizon when Cap stirred. Awake, he lost no time in preparing for the day and was satisfied to eat biscuit and jerky washed down with water from his canteen as he dare not risk a fire.

He hoped that sleep had not brought a change of mind to Pecos, and he started to put into operation the plan he had made before he slept. After he had eliminated all signs of his night stay, he rode for three miles in the direction of Mather and positioned himself on a rise from which he could view the land towards Durango. He drew his spyglass and studied the distance for any movement. Nothing. By now the sun was beginning to climb. Under its intensifying light he continued to watch in the direction of the night camp near the rocks.

No movement. Maybe they had been awake early and were long gone. Pecos must have decided to go to Durango with Dutch and Jake. So much for his first hope of revenge. But Cap waited. He had no need to hurry. He knew the men he wanted were going to Durango.

The minutes passed, and with them Cap's concentration faltered. Suddenly he started. Something moved. He stared into the distance. Nothing. He had been mistaken. His imagination playing tricks.

He raised his spyglass to his eye and swept his gaze across the land where he thought he had seen a movement. Nothing. He stopped. Instinct told him he had missed something. He moved his gaze back more slowly. Yes. There! Someone crouched by a horse examining its hoof. The man stood, patted the horse's neck and swung into the saddle. He headed in Cap's direction. Pecos! Heading for Mather just as Cap hoped he would.

Cap hurried to his horse and rode quickly to the rocky area which cut across the trail. He hid his horse and positioned himself so that he had a view of the trail for about half a mile.

The clop of a horse's hoofs, approaching at a steady pace, alerted Cap. He drew his Colt and watched Pecos coming nearer and nearer.

Cap's sudden appearance so startled Pecos that he automatically checked his horse.

'Hold it!' rapped Cap as he saw the instinctive movement of a hand towards a holstered gun.

Pecos froze.

'Step down. Easy.' There was a warning and a threat behind Cap's final word.

Pecos swung slowly from the saddle, his dark eyes watching Cap with cold hatred.

'Step away from your horse,' ordered Cap.

Pecos moved to one side.

Cap saw the alertness in Pecos's eyes search for some means to extract himself from this situation. And he saw that change to fear as he stepped towards him. Cap stopped less than an arm's length from Pecos.

'So I was right, you did go back to Mather,' said Pecos.

'Sure. I had to know what had happened

to Rusty.'

Cap swung his Colt up suddenly and brought the barrel hard down Pecos's left cheek, leaving a huge gash which poured blood. Pecos staggered, grasping at his wound.

'Like it?' hissed Cap. 'Like what you gave him?'

Pecos crouched, his eyes smouldering with venomous hate.

Cap slashed his Colt across the fingers holding the cheek. Pecos's right hand grabbed his left trying to relieve the agony. He was unprepared for the knee driven hard into his groin. He yelled at the excruciating pain, doubled up and fell on to his knees. Cap drove his left fist hard into Pecos's back between his shoulders, pitching him forward. Instinctively his hands went forward to save himself. As they sprawled in front of him Cap drove his foot hard down on to Pecos's left hand and ground the fingers viciously.

Pecos screamed.

'For Rusty,' Cap yelled, and stamped hard again.

As he stepped back, Pecos rolled over. His face was creased with suffering, but through it burned a hate which Cap knew could erupt any moment. Pecos had been driven almost to the point where he would take desperate action. Cap had judged his man correctly. He had purposely left Pecos's right hand untouched and his gun in its holster.

'Get up,' snapped Cap. 'You ain't had as much as Rusty yet.'

Pecos glared at Cap but made no attempt to rise. Cap fired, spurting the dust close to Pecos's ear.

'Up!' Cap's order sounded above the crash of the shot still reverberating round the rocks.

Pecos moved slowly, watching Cap with hatred in eyes which also sought one tiny chink in Cap's watchful stance. And Cap knew it. He reached out with his left hand, but Pecos swayed out of reach. He staggered. Cap slipped his Colt back into its holster, and started to reach again.

The moment Pecos had been waiting for! He straightened, his hand clawing at the butt of his Colt. Exactly as Cap had anticipated. His gun was back in his hand almost before Pecos's had cleared its leather.

Cap's finger closed around the trigger. The bullet took Pecos in the chest, blasting him backwards. For one brief moment there was an incredulous look on his face, and then it was gone. He hit the ground and lay still. Cap eyed him with disdain.

'One for you, Rusty,' he muttered.

11

Cap waited a mile out of Durango until it was dusk. He had ridden all day to make sure he reached the town that night. He did not expect Cole for two days, but he wanted to be there in case there was a change of plan. Nothing must destroy the lead that he had; lose contact with Cole now and the chance of picking him up again might never come.

Besides he had a surprise for Jake and Dutch. A surprise which would shock them. And shocked men became nervous. In a nervous state men became more predictable in their actions for they did not think coolly.

When Cap saw the lights begin to appear in a number of the buildings in Durango, he rode forward slowly until he reached the edge of town. He sat motionless for a few moments. He wanted no movement to betray his presence. He studied the main street. There was no one about unless they were lurking in the shadows. A medley of sounds rose from the saloon. Cap waited.

The time seemed endless, but he was a patient man when it came to implementing a scheme from which he hoped he would benefit. Five minutes passed before he saw what he wanted. Two men walked along the sidewalk, their presence emphasised when they passed through the light allowed to mark the boards by uncurtained windows.

Cap tugged at the long rein he held in his left hand. A horse moved forward and, when it reached him, Cap tossed the reins over the prone figure slung face downwards across the saddle. He tapped the animal on its rump and it continued its walk into Durango. Cap watched to make certain the horse neither stopped nor turned round. As it passed the first buildings, Cap sent his own horse forward, but deviated to the right to the first house which he had noticed on his arrival was deserted and dilapidated.

He moved round to the back, every nerve alerted, his ears tuned to pick up the slightest sound which would indicate some-one was about. But no such sound came. Cap slid from the saddle, secured his horse close to the back door of the building. The door squeaked on its rusty hinges as Cap pushed it open. He paused and listened. Nothing, only the distant hum coming from the saloon. With Colt drawn Cap moved swiftly to the front room of the house. When he found that the broken window did not afford him the view he wanted he went swiftly upstairs.

Entering a room at the front he was satis-fied that it allowed him to see along the main street with a good aspect of the saloon. The two men still walked on the sidewalk. The horse plodded further and further along the dust street.

Suddenly the two men stopped, glanced at each other and then started to run towards the horse. At the sudden clatter the horse hesitated, and at the sight of the two men jumping down from the sidewalk it moved nervously away from them. It started to run but, before it could get any speed, one of the men grabbed the trailing reins while the other one went to the horse's head. They soothed it under control, and when it was standing calmly, the man with the reins came to the body. He raised the head by its hair and peered at the face. He released his hold, said something to his companion and they led the horse quickly to the hitching-rail outside the saloon.

Cap saw them hurry inside, and a few moments later they emerged with two others whom he guessed were Dutch and Jake.

The shock of identifying Pecos for themselves finally cleared the alcoholic haze which had been penetrated when the news came into the saloon. They glanced nervously at each other, each knowing the words which blazed in the other's mind – Cap Millet!

They looked up and down the street and then turned to the men who had brought the news.

'Did you see anyone with this horse?' asked Dutch.

'No. We were coming to the saloon and the horse came out of the darkness.'

'Millet must have brought it. He's out there.' There was a tremor in Jake's voice and his hand hovered over the butt of his Colt. 'I'll get him, finish him once and for all.' His was the bravado of the nervous. He started forward, but was half glad when Dutch gripped him with a restraining hand.

'Don't be a fool,' hissed Dutch. 'That's just what he wants us to do. He's probably watching us now, ready to pick us off when we get near him.'

'Guess you're right,' returned Jake.

'As long as we stay here we're safe. He won't come into town, and before daylight comes he'll realise his ruse has failed and he'll be long gone. He won't want to be around Durango.' Dutch turned Jake back towards the saloon.

The knot of men and saloon girls who had

come on to the sidewalk, as the news had spread, parted. Dutch paused to have a word with a small, tubby man. The man nodded, scurried down the steps and led the horse away.

When they had replenished their drinks Jake spoke. 'I'm not so sure about Millet being long gone tomorrow. I figure he'll be somewhere out there watching, waiting for our next move.'

'You want to go see in the morning, and if you're right finish up like Pecos? He played a hunch that Millet would go back to Rusty. Seems he was right, and look where it got him.'

'I wasn't figuring on looking for him. But I reckon Cole should be warned.'

Dutch looked thoughtful, considering the situation. 'Maybe you're right. If Millet spots Cole on his own he'll try to take him, and if he succeeds we're going to lose out on what-ever Cole has in mind. If we ride together to meet Cole, Millet won't dare try anything.'

The two men settled down to their drinks

wondering if Millet was still somewhere out there in the darkness.

When Cap saw everyone return to the salon he considered it unlikely that Dutch and Jake would make a move that night. Maybe they would just wait for Cole to arrive. Cap wanted action before that and decided that the two men might need a little gentle persuasion. He waited half an hour, giving their minds time to settle after the jolt they had received.

Cap left the house, using the utmost caution. Keeping to the shadows he made his way along the sidewalks, meeting no one. He paused almost opposite the saloon and strained his eyes against the darkness to survey both street and his immediate surrounds. There was no one about. Cap stepped swiftly off the sidewalk and hurried quickly across the street, alert to any other presence, should anyone appear. Reaching the opposite side of the roadway he entered the alley by the side of the saloon, pleased of the darkness to cloak him.

He reached the outside stairs which acted as a fire escape for the upper floor. He mounted them quickly and tried the door. It resisted his pressure. He tested the panel closest to the lock. It gave a little. A sharp blow might do it. He pulled his Colt from its holster and gripped it round the chamber, turning the butt hammerlike. He hesitated. Footsteps on the sidewalk. He concentrated his gaze on the main street. The footsteps grew louder and he made out the blackness of a figure as someone passed the end of the alley. He waited until the footsteps faded.

Turning his attention back to the door he gave the panel a sharp, forceful blow. Wood splintered in what, to Cap, sounded a thunderous explosion. He froze, every nerve taut, ready to evade the curiosity he must have aroused.

But no signs of alarm or investigation reached him. He pushed at the splintered wood, carefully breaking a piece off here, prising a splinter back there, until he was able to insert his hand and reach to the key he knew would be there if the door was to serve a use in the case of a fire.

He turned the key and pushed the door open. All was quiet on the dimly lit corridor. The only sound came from the saloon below. Cap stepped to the first door on his right, turned the knob slowly and pushed gently. It was locked. Four steps took him to the next door. This one yielded. Cap thrust it open and stepped inside quickly.

'Bob, I–'The words froze on the lips of the girl, who sat preening her hair in front of a mirror, when she saw Cap's reflection. 'What the hell?' she said, swinging round on her chair, flicking her flimsy gown across her nakedness.

'Hold it!' rapped Cap, firmly but gently. 'I only want a favour.'

'You'll have to take your turn in the queue,' returned the girl indignantly. 'Now git before Bob gives you a heap of trouble.'

'All right, I'm going,' returned Cap. 'I only want you to deliver a message for me.' He was fishing in his pocket as he spoke. He drew out a roll of notes, peeled off four and held them out. The girl's eyes drifted from them to Cap.

'That to deliver a message,' the girl smiled. 'I'll throw in something else if you hang around.'

'Can't do that,' replied Cap.

The girl reached out and took the notes. 'What do you want me to do?' she asked over her shoulder as she half turned and stuffed them into a drawer.

'Go to Jake and Dutch, they're in the saloon, and tell them Cap Millet will be seeing them.'

The girl's eyes widened. 'You – I heard them use that name when they saw Pecos. You–' Her stuttered words died away.

'It's all right,' Cap reassured her. 'Just deliver that message as soon as I've gone. That's all you have to do.'

The girl had regained her composure. She had been in some tight corners, dealt with some rough cowboys, but this one seemed genuine.

'Sure,' she said, getting to her feet. 'Certain you ain't interested in anything else?' Her gown parted.

'Certain,' replied Cap with a wry smile.

'Sure is the easiest money I've ever earned.' She turned with her back to Cap and let the gown slip from her shoulders as she reached for a dress.

'Give me time to get to the bottom of the outside steps,' said Cap.

'You'll be down by the time I get some stockings on,' she replied as she slipped the dress over her head.

'Thanks,' said Cap.

'Any time, fella, for anything.'

Cap eased the door and glanced into the corridor. He stepped outside quickly and hurried to the fire escape. He reached the bottom, ran to the end of the alley farthest from the main street and waited.

When the girl reached the stairs leading into the saloon, she paused to survey the occupants below. Bob was halfway up the stairs.

'Hi, honey, I thought you and I–' he started.

'Sure,' she replied. 'I just have a job to do. I'll be back in a minute.' She stepped past him and started down the stairs.

'Don't be long, Kitty,' Bob called after her.

'I won't,' she assured him with a tantalising smile over her shoulder. She turned her attention to the saloon and crossed the floor to the bar. When she tapped Dutch and Jake on the shoulders they both turned round. 'Got a message for you fellas. Cap Millet says he'll be seeing you.'

For a moment the significance of her words did not seem to register, then, as they made their impact, both men exploded. 'What!' They glanced at each other in disbelief.

'Cap Millet said he'd be seeing you,' Kitty repeated.

Jake was the first to recover from his surprise. 'When did you see him?' he rapped.

'A few minutes ago in my room,' replied Kitty. 'Came up the outside stairs. Left the same way.'

'Come on, Dutch,' called Jake, and ran for the batwings.

The sudden movement jerked Dutch back to reality. 'Wait,' he shouted, but Jake ignored him. Dutch raced after his friend.

Jake left the batwings swinging viciously behind him. He stood on the sidewalk, Colt in hand, turning his head from left to right and back again, searching for the man who had sent the message.

Dutch pulled up alongside him as he burst from the saloon.

'Careful, Jake,' he snapped. 'Maybe Millet wants us outside.'

Jake glared at his companion. 'He's not far away and we can get him, finish him.' The notes of a frightened man were in his voice.

Dutch realised it. 'Get a hold on yourself!' he rapped. 'Can't you see this is what he wants?'

'He's in town,' snarled Jake. 'We can finish him. We've enough guns in the saloon who'll help us flush him out. Unless you're too scared to help!'

The taunt needled Dutch and fogged his judgement. 'Hell I am.'

'He ain't on the street, so he must have used the alley. I'll check it while you get some guns to back us, then we'll search the town from end to end. That hombre sure won't leave Durango alive.' Without waiting to hear from Dutch, Jake ran to the alley and disappeared round the corner.

Dutch hesitated a moment. Should he go after Jake? But Millet was hardly likely to linger in the alley. Better rustle up some help. Dutch turned and swung back through the batwings.

Jake, straining under the nervous tension which gripped his body, hurried along the alley. He keyed himself for any sound which might betray Millet's presence. He reached the end of the alley and stopped.

'Looking for me?' a voice called from out of the darkness of the narrow back street which ran to his left.

Jake swung round, his Colt ready, every

nerve bristling.

All was quiet. Then the sound of running feet broke the silence. Jake started after them. Millet was heading for the edge of town. He must have a horse there. Jake renewed his effort. Millet must not get away. The sound of the running suddenly became less distinct. Millet had turned. Reaching the next crossing, Jake hesitated only long enough to realize that Millet was racing for the main street. He grinned to himself. If Dutch had been quick enough there would be men on the street who would spot the man they were after.

The footsteps ahead faltered, then ran on. Jake drove himself hard. He must have gained through that pause. Suddenly he ran into a hard object which took him at knee height, sending him sprawling. He cursed as he pushed himself up only to stumble again over the barrel which Cap had tipped on to its side.

Jake's upending gave Cap the few moments he needed to check the main street. Seeing no one, Cap raced across the open roadway and gained the other side.

When Jake reached the street there was still no one from the saloon. Jake cursed. What the hell was Dutch doing? Jake didn't want to lose touch with Millet and there was only one way he must have gone – straight across the street. Jake ran on.

The moonlight failed to penetrate the darkness of the alley, but Jake, wanting to keep contact with his quarry, hurried on. He heard the sound of footsteps beyond the corner and was drawn by them into rounding it without hesitation. He pulled up with a start when he almost collided with someone. He felt the hard muzzle of a Colt driven into his ribs. Jake cursed.

'Drop your gun,' hissed Cap.

The dull thud told him that he had been obeyed. Cap stepped to one side and said, 'March. End house.'

Jake hesitated, but the touch of metal in his side changed his mind.

'Inside,' rapped Cap when they reached

the house. 'Where's Dutch?' he asked as they went into the front room.

The light from the moon revealed the smile which flicked Jake's lips at the mention of Dutch.

'He'll have all the men in the saloon looking for you now. They'll search every building. You'll not get away.'

'Then I'd better finish my business quickly,' answered Cap.

'I can't tell you anything. Cole made the deal about hanging you. I know nothing.'

'Sure,' agreed Cap. 'I ain't talking about that. Cole will tell me. It's Rusty I'm thinking about.'

Horror came to Jake's eyes. He remembered Pecos. 'I had nothing to do with that,' protested Jake, a tremor in his voice.

'Liar!' snapped Cap. 'You were all responsible. Someone had to hold his hands while his nails were prised.' Cap's voice trailed away with the realisation of who must have used the knife. 'You! You're the knife man!' Cap struck viciously with his Colt. But the sudden anger distorted his concentration.

Jake, who had been watching Cap intently, saw the blow coming. He twisted to one side and took the gun on his upper arm. With his mind focused on escape he was almost oblivious to the pain. His right hand slid inside his shirt and in the same movement withdrew his knife. He lunged at Cap. Cap swayed. The knife ripped his shirt and nicked his side. Jake grappled and the weight of his impact sent them crashing to the floor. Cap lost the grip on his Colt, and the gun spun across the floor. He drove his knee upwards and at the same time pushed against Jake's shoulders with all his strength. As Jake fell sideways, Cap rolled over, grasping for the hand which held the knife. His left hand closed around Jake's wrist.

Jake clawed at Cap's face, but, in spite of the torn flesh, Cap did not relinquish his grip. Jake heaved, throwing Cap to one side, and Cap, still holding the wrist, took him with him. Jake threw all his weight on Cap, pinning him to the floor. He exerted more strength in his arm and slowly started to bring the knife over and closer to Cap. Jake gritted his teeth, his face contorted as he built up the pressure. Cap strained his resistance. The knife came closer. It was poised above him. One extra push which he could not resist and he would be finished. Cap fought with all his strength. He swung his free arm at Jake, but the blow was not powerful enough to release Jake's pressure. The knife gleamed in the moonlight, poised for its moment of destruction.

Jake's eyes fired with triumph. He'd finish what the rope had failed to do.

Cap relaxed his grip for a fraction of a split second, and in so doing released some of the pressure exerted by Jake. The immediate retention on his wrist took Jake by surprise so that, before he could remuster his full strength, Cap had forced his arm back and over. Jake's body went with it and he could not escape the knife. His full weight drove the knife deep. He stiffened, his eyes wide with disbelief. He jerked, then slackened.

He lay still. His eyes stared without seeing.

Cap, his chest heaving with the exertion, pushed himself to his feet and gazed at the dead man. 'Another for you, Rusty,' he muttered.

Distant shouts penetrated his bemused mind. Dutch had men looking for him. He must move quickly. He retrieved his gun and hurried to the back door. He stepped outside with caution and ran to his horse. Once he was in the saddle he sent the animal away from Durango at a fast gallop. There was no need to hide his presence. The men who searched for him were not mounted, and he would be far gone before they could saddle their horses. He heard shouts renewed along the street and he knew that before many minutes Dutch would know Jake's fate.

They had both reacted as he had expected to the message he sent with the saloon girl. Now, if he surmised correctly, Dutch would want to warn Cole.

12

Cap doubted if there would be any pursuit, but he was cautious and rode for ten miles before stopping. He rested his horse while he had some food and then returned in the direction of Durango. He found a suitable place from which he could view the town when daylight came, and, after unsaddling his horse, he settled down for the rest of the night. Sleep came quickly and heavily, but his inner sense woke him before daybreak.

After tending to his horse and making his breakfast he destroyed all evidence of his night stop. By the time Durango was flooded with the morning light Cap Millet, with his horse saddled, was on watch.

An hour later his supposition about Dutch's reactions was rewarded. The man rode out of Durango at a steady pace along the west trail. Cap climbed into the saddle and matched Dutch's pace on a parallel course from which he could keep his man in sight without betraying his presence.

Dutch rode until mid-afternoon when he halted beside a river ford. From the cover of the higher ground, some half-mile from the river, Cap watched him make camp.

Studying the terrain beyond the river Cap understood the reason why Dutch had chosen this site to make camp. On the far bank three trails converged on the ford. Dutch must not know which one Cole would use from Pincher Creek.

The following morning was moving slowly towards noon when Cap sighted a lone rider coming at an easy pace along the right-hand trail at the far side of the river. Cap raised his spyglass and focused it on the man. Cole! The man who had the answers he wanted. Tension gripped Cap.

Should he try for them here or await developments? He was curious about the 'big killing' which Cole had planned. It had come so soon after the attempted hanging that Cap wondered if the two were connected. He decided to wait.

He turned his attention to Dutch. The man, who had cleared his camp early in the morning, still sat close to the ford. He was not aware yet of Cole's approach.

Cap kept his spyglass trained on Dutch. A few minutes later he saw him stiffen and incline his head as if listening. A moment passed, then he scrambled to his feet and moved so he could sight the right-hand trail better.

When Cole saw Dutch across the river he was irritated. He had said he would see his sidekicks in Durango, so what the hell was Dutch doing here? He put his horse to the water where its swifter flow was slackened by the extra width between its banks. The animal splashed through the water and mounted the low bank to be halted by its rider close to Dutch.

'Why you here?' demanded Cole as he swung from the saddle. 'Where's Jake and

Pecos? Back in Durango where you should be?'

'Dead!'

'What!' Cole stated incredulously at Dutch.

'Millet got 'em. I came out here to warn you. Thought you ought to know as soon as possible. I didn't know which trail you took from Pincher Creek so waited here.'

'What the hell happened?' snapped Cole.

Dutch gave him the story. 'Does this upset the plans you have in mind?' asked Dutch when he had passed all the information to Cole.

Cole, his mouth tight in a grim line, looked thoughtful for a few moments.

'No. Just means more for us.' The idea of that wiped the serious expression from his face. 'Maybe Millet did us a good turn.'

'What you been working on?' asked Dutch, glad to have Cole's calming effect on a situation which had made him edgy.

'You'll learn in good time. What I found out in Pincher Creek confirmed my suspicions. Three days' ride and we'll use the knowledge to gain us a fortune.' The grin broadened on his face. Suddenly it vanished and the stern expression of concern startled Dutch. 'You sure Millet hasn't trailed you?' He glanced around as if expecting to see Cap.

''Course not,' replied Dutch. 'I reckon he was scared off by all the guns we had looking for him in Durango. He lit out of there as if the devil was chasing him. So he was out of sight before some of us saddled up, but we rode five miles along the trail he took without any sight of him.'

'I sure hope you're right, 'cos I reckon he won't be satisfied with just Pecos and Jake.'

'Hell, if he'd doubled back and followed me he could have picked me off here any time.'

'Maybe he knew you were meeting me, so you were his lead.'

'How the hell could he know? But, suppose he did, he needn't have waited until you showed up. He could have got rid of me and then waited for you.'

Cole nodded thoughtfully. 'Guess so,' he muttered. 'He's picked up our trail in Durango twice, so maybe he'll figure we'll be there again. Well, we won't. And when my plans work out we'll be far gone. He'll never know where we are.' He grinned. 'Let's ride, Dutch.'

The two men mounted their horses and crossed the river.

Cap watched them break into a steady trot, and when he reckoned they were a safe distance ahead he followed.

Late in the afternoon the two men made camp and, after he was sure that they were settled for the night, Cap did likewise.

The same pattern was followed the next day.

Cole and Dutch were on the trail early the third morning, and by noon Cap recognised some of the countryside. They were near Claystone and to Cap this was hanging country!

Why had Cole and Dutch returned here, a

place they had avoided for five years between leaving Fletcher's employment and the attempted hanging? Was there any significance in this? Was this where Cole reckoned he was going to make a 'big killing'?

Cap sharpened his pace to close the distance between himself and his quarry. He did not want to lose contact now.

Cap's curiosity was roused even further when he realised they were heading for Dan Fletcher's Lazy A. Had he hired Cole and his sidekicks for another job? Was Fletcher involved in Cole's plans? When Cap saw Cole call a halt and the two men settle down in the shade of some rocks just off the trail, he figured they hadn't been hired by Fletcher. If they had why wait here? Unless the meeting with Fletcher had to be unknown to anyone else.

Cap studied the landscape and figured a route which would enable him to get closer to the two men. He turned his horse off the trail and circled to his left. He dropped into a dried-out arroyo which afforded him cover until he was on the opposite side of the rocks to the trail and completely hidden from Cole and Dutch.

He left his horse and, using every available cover, made his way towards the rocks. Reaching them he exercised the utmost caution, pausing every few moments to catch the sound of voices. Once he was able to distinguish words, Cap stopped.

'–so we wait.' It was Dutch's voice.

'Yeah, the fewer cowpokes about the better. They'll be heading for a night in Claystone and then we can go in and see Fletcher,' said Cole.

'What put you on to this?' asked Dutch.

'I played a hunch and decided to make a few enquiries. They paid off.'

Cap cursed his luck. He was too late to gain any information. Cole had already briefed Dutch.

The conversation dwindled and, when Cap realised he would learn no more, he slipped back to the arroyo. He knew that Cole and Dutch were going to visit Fletcher and he figured it might be advantageous if he could learn the reason for that visit.

He led his horse along the arroyo until he reached a point from which he could survey the land as far as the Lazy A ranch house.

He needed to approach the house from the rear and saw his chance to do so by using the cover of a ridge which rose gradually from the trail and curved behind the ranch buildings.

Three times he left his horse and went on foot to the top of the ridge to study his position, and three times he rode on. The fourth survey satisfied him and he settled down to await the arrival of Cole and Dutch.

He saw the ranch-hands ride out with raucous shouts and laughter bent on a night of enjoyment in Claystone. Ten minutes later Cole and Dutch appeared riding at a steady pace towards the house.

When they passed from his view in front of the building, Cap slipped from the ridge and started down the gentle slope. Every nerve was alert, his eyes roving, seeking anything which would indicate that he had been seen.

He reached the back of the house without mishap, flattened himself against the wall and paused to listen. No sound. He moved quickly to the back door and very carefully turned the knob. He pushed gently. The door wasn't locked. Cap drew his Colt and thrust the door open, stepping inside immediately. No one was there. Cap closed the door gently behind him. He crossed the kitchen to the door which led into the house. He eased it ajar and heard voices coming from a room on the right-hand side of the corridor.

'Just tell Mr Fletcher we want to see him.' Cole's voice carried the tone of an order.

'He told me he didn't want disturbing.' Cap recognised Jed Carson's voice even though his interview with him had been brief.

'Get him!' rapped Cole.

'Why are you back here after five years? We have nothing more for you.'

'But I have for Fletcher. Now get him!'

'I'm sure he'd want me to deal with it.'

'He wouldn't.' There was a half laugh in Cole's voice. 'Now are you going to get him or do I raise such hell that he'll come?'

'All right. I'll see what he says, but I can't guarantee that he will,' replied Jed, still trying to put Cole off.

'He'll come.'

Cap heard footsteps, and from his position he saw Carson cross the hallway at the far end of the corridor and go up the stairs. A few minutes later Cap heard two sets of footsteps coming down the stairs, and a man he judged to be Fletcher, followed by Carson, crossed his vision.

For a moment they were only impressions, then something clicked in the back of Cap's mind. He had seen Fletcher somewhere. But where? When? Fletcher? He knew no one of that name. Cap churned his mind, seeking an answer. Maybe he was mistaken. Fletcher must have reminded him of someone. Harsh words broke into his racing thoughts.

'What the hell are you doing here?' It was a voice Cap did not recognise and he presumed it was Fletcher's.

'We have some talking to do,' replied Cole.

'I've nothing to talk to you about,' returned Fletcher.

'I figure we have,' rapped Cole.

'You heard Mr Fletcher,' cut in Jed harshly. 'He wants you out, so git.'

'Hold it!' rapped Dutch. 'Keep your hand away from that gun.'

'Ease it, Jed,' instructed Fletcher, cooling the situation.

Jed was puzzled. The last job Cole had done for Fletcher was five years ago. Had they been hired to do another job unknown to him? Was it connected with Millet? He recalled how Fletcher had been taken aback when he had told him of Millet's visit. He remembered how Fletcher's questions about that visit had been searching while trying to appear casual. He recalled how his own enquiry asking if Dan knew Millet had brought a denial and sharp rebuff. Fletcher had been edgy for a few days.

Jed moved his hand away from his gun.

'All right, what have you to say that I'll be interested in?' asked Fletcher.

'Want him to hear?' asked Cole, indicating Carson.

'He's like a son to me so anything you have to say can be said in front of him.'

'You sure?'

'Damn you, man. Get on with it. Say what you have to say and get out.'

'Concerns the last job we did for you.' Cole grinned at the startled look which came to Fletcher's face. 'Still want him to stay?' Fletcher hesitated. He appeared to be going to change his mind when Cole spoke again. 'Maybe it is better if he stays and hears what I have to say.' Cole had realised that he might be able to use the fact of Jed's presence to advantage.

'Get on,' rapped Fletcher irritably.

'I got curious about the last job and made some investigations,' explained Cole. He noted with satisfaction the gleam of alarm in Fletcher's eyes. 'Giving us notes on two banks as well as cash got me wondering. I reckoned the cash had come from the bank in Claystone. Three bank accounts. Why? No point unless you had so much you didn't want to risk it all in one place.' He paused, letting the information sink in.

'Go on.' Fletcher's voice had a slight note of resignation in it, as if he knew what was coming.

'Well, like I said, I made some enquiries. Bribing bank clerks was easy after what you paid us for the job.' Cole laughed. 'Funny how your money has helped us to get to you.'

'Damn you, get to the point. What is it you want?'

'All in good time, Mr Fletcher.' Cole was relishing in the knowledge he had but he needed to play Fletcher along into admitting that what he was surmising was correct. He couldn't prove the final and vital point so he must force Fletcher into verifying it. 'Apart from telling me the size of your accounts and the fact that they believed that you also used three other banks, they were able to tell me that the accounts were opened within six months of the war ending.'

'Damn them, I'll have them sacked.'

'Will you?' sneered Cole. 'If you do I'll tell the authorities all I know.'

'And just what do you know?' asked Fletcher with an element of doubt. 'All you've told me is that I have a number of bank accounts and that I opened them after the war.'

'Very soon after the war,' replied Cole. 'And you bought this ranch. That would mean a huge sum of money for someone to be handling so soon after hostilities. It got me thinking. I recalled a shipment of money which went missing during the war. Union troops were moving it and were ambushed by the Feds. A group of troopers under one officer broke out of the ambush with the money. Some of the Confederate troops went after them. Seems they caught up with them. Only the Union officer survived.'

'So what's all this to do with me?' demanded Fletcher.

'All in good time. This officer said the Feds had got the money, but after the war the Feds denied it.'

'So, their troopers kept it for themselves,' said Fletcher.

'They didn't.' Cole spoke quietly as he shook his head. 'I know because I was one of the Feds at the main ambush. When we finally wiped out all the Yankees we found our party, who went after the money, were all dead. So we assumed the money had reached the Union.'

He was watching Fletcher very carefully. He could prove little beyond this point. Now he needed an admission. He hit hard with his statements, making his suppositions sound like facts, as if he had proof of everything he said. 'The surviving officer was called Rogers. He had the money. Hid it. Recovered it after the war. Came to Claystone. Bought this ranch. Banked the rest and changed his name to Fletcher!'

The momentary flash which crossed Fletcher's eyes told Cole he was right, but Fletcher was quick to recover his composure. He laughed loud. 'Hell, you've got a vivid imagination, Cole. Just because I'm rich you associate me with that episode during the war. Even if it was right you couldn't prove it.'

'It's right,' snapped Cole. 'Why should you want us to get rid of Cap Millet in a way which would not raise any enquiries? Wasn't he the investigating officer into the loss of the money? Isn't that why you wanted him out of the way? Weren't you afraid he might recognise you, and the fact that you had prospered so readily might set him wondering?'

Dan saw the startled look which had come to Jed's eyes. He knew that Jed was linking this information with Millet's visit and with the rope-burn he had seen on Millet's neck, and that he realised Cole's facts were near the truth and that Dan had lied when he had denied knowing Millet. It was no use trying to disguise the fact any longer.

'All right,' rapped Fletcher. 'So you've investigated and guessed. What do you want?'

Cole smirked. He had Fletcher where he wanted him. Now he could move in for the big kill. 'Let's settle for half your assets.'

'What!' Fletcher was astounded by the audacity of the man. 'Not likely. I paid you well to get rid of Millet but you made a mess of it.'

Cole showed surprise, and Fletcher seized on it.

'Oh, yes, I know. Millet came here after the hanging. Seems a young fella cut him down in time and that youngster recognised his description of you and told him you had worked for me five years ago. Millet came here trying to get a lead. I wasn't here, but Jed told him what he knew about you.'

'So that's how Millet got on our trail,' hissed Cole.

'Did he get near you?' There was a touch of alarm in Fletcher's voice.

'Near enough to kill Pecos and Jake,' put in Dutch.

'Hell! So he could have followed you here!'

'No,' said Cole. 'Pecos was killed on his way back to Mather alone. He got Jake in Durango, but, with Dutch and a posse after him, he hightailed it. Dutch met me out of Durango and warned me, so we avoided Durango in case he'd doubled back expecting me to meet up with Dutch there. You can rest easy, he ain't followed us here. So we can close our deal. Dutch and I will lose ourselves way north and Millet will never know that Dan Fletcher was really Lieutenant Rogers who made good with Union gold.'

'You won't be going anywhere,' Cap's voice was quietly menacing as he pushed open the door and stepped into the room.

13

Dutch was the first to react to the startling intrusion. He still held his Colt after Jed's attempted interference. He swung round, but, even as he was squeezing the trigger, a bullet from Cap's Colt drove life from him.

'For Rusty,' muttered Cap as Dutch crashed to the floor. 'Leave it!' he rapped loudly when he saw Cole make a move for his gun.

'Hell, thought you hadn't been followed,' Fletcher snarled through the shock of seeing Cap.

Cole cursed Cap.

'Never figured that trailing them to find out why they tried to hang me would lead me here, and take me back to the war,' said Cap. 'I've been in the kitchen, saw you cross the hall, you were familiar but I couldn't place you until Cole told his story. I reckon he was only guessing about you being Rogers. Don't see how he could have got proof of that.'

Fletcher turned on Cole. His eyes blazed with a furious hate. 'Is that true?' he snarled.

'I had to get you to admit it,' rapped Cole.

'Damn you!' Fletcher could see his world collapsing. Cap Millet, who had come so very near the truth in his investigations as a Union officer, now had heard his admission. Hatred flowed from him and hatred brought a desperation to survive in the world he had made. Get rid of the only witness and it would be his word against Millet's. Jed wouldn't testify against him. His hand flashed for his gun. It cleared its leather, but Cole was that shade faster and the bullet took the rancher in the stomach, pitching him against the wall, his own bullet crashing harmlessly into the floor. Cole swung in the same movement, but, before he could squeeze the trigger again, Cap fired. Cole's eyes widened. He staggered backwards, doubled and pitched to the floor.

'For Rusty and for me,' Cap whispered. He turned to Fletcher. Jed was on his knees beside him.

'He ain't dead, we've got to get the doc quickly,' cried Jed over his shoulder. He started to rise to his feet.

'Hold it, Jed,' gasped Fletcher. 'It's no good. I'm done for. Maybe just as well. Never expected this fella to come looking for me.' He indicated Cap. 'I couldn't have faced the truth coming out.'

'I wasn't looking for you, Rogers. I was just drifting.'

Fletcher swallowed hard. 'So if I hadn't seen you hole up with a lame horse none of this would have happened.' He gave a hollow laugh which started him coughing. 'Sorry you learned the truth about me, Jed.' He gasped the words slowly, each one getting fainter.

'I never knew a man called Rogers,' replied Jed. 'I only knew a man called Fletcher who ran the Lazy A efficiently and was good to me.'

The publishers hope that this book has given you enjoyable reading. Large Print Books are especially designed to be as easy to see and hold as possible. If you wish a complete list of our books please ask at your local library or write directly to:

Dales Large Print Books
Magna House, Long Preston,
Skipton, North Yorkshire.
BD23 4ND

This Large Print Book, for people
who cannot read normal print,
is published under the auspices of
THE ULVERSCROFT FOUNDATION